CRIME BEFORE CHRISTMAS

A Bookish Cafe Mystery Book 4

HARPER LIN

This is a work of fiction. Names, characters, organizations, places, events, and incidents are either products of the author's imagination or are used fictitiously.

Crime Before Christmas

ISBN: 978-1-987859-88-1

www.harperlin.com

Chapter 1

The multicolored string of lights just didn't want to cooperate this year. Maggie Bell struggled to keep them from tangling as she strung them around the outside of her front door.

"What the heck," she muttered. "The window at work looks perfect and has a million more lights than this. Why can't I get this right?"

It wasn't the lights that were causing her trouble. If she thought back, she'd had to untangle them as she strung them just about every year. But last year, Mr. Alexander Whitfield, her boss, had still been alive. They had had a tradition of spending the days leading up to Christmas reading old children's stories about Jolly St. Nick or Krampus and never neglected the story that started it all with a star in the sky and a small manger. But this year, she was afraid to even look at the books they'd read and discussed at length together.

After letting the string fall from her hands and dangle around the door, Maggie let out a deep sigh. She turned around to look at her landlord's house and shook her head. Mrs. Peacock was determined to win the house-decorating contest and steal the trophy away from her nemesis, Mrs. Donovan, who lived a few doors down. The place looked like an amusement park. There were a full-size Santa and sleigh on the roof. A complete Nativity stood in the front yard. To keep the baby Jesus company, there were Snoopy, Frosty, and an army of other festive characters wearing wreaths around their necks or mummified with red and green lights.

Maggie didn't want her little cottage to look like a mausoleum in the backyard. Had she not done something, it would appear like a black hole in the yard among the thousands of twinkling lights on the main house. So she always strung up something to make Mrs. Peacock happy. Normally, she liked it. It was a tradition that got the holiday juices flowing. But this year was different.

Not only was Mr. Whitfield gone, but it seemed as if her usual anticipation for the holiday was gone too. As she stood there looking at the knotted lights, she pouted and furrowed her brow. Tears came to her eyes, and she was about to burst out crying when she heard footsteps. Quickly, she looked to her left to see the last face she wanted to see but the one she always missed the most.

"Hey, that's looking good," Joshua Whitfield said as he walked up the salted sidewalk to Maggie's house.

"Thanks," Maggie said before she quickly bit down on her tongue and forced her emotions back down. "I thought maybe this year, I'd give Mrs. Peacock a run for her money."

Joshua looked over his shoulder at Mrs. Peacock's house and chuckled. "It looks like she's trying to help jumbo jets land with all those lights."

"Mrs. Donovan won the house decorating contest last year. There's no way Mrs. Peacock is going to let that happen two years in a row," Maggie said and reluctantly picked up the knotted end of the string of lights.

"Here, let me help you with that," Joshua said and took the angry ball of tangles from her.

Maggie let out a deep sigh. She hated being

helped, but she hated it more when she really needed it.

"What are you doing out here?" Maggie asked. "You only get Thursday night off. I wouldn't be spending it roaming the streets of Fair Haven when the weather is calling for snow."

"Actually, I was getting into the Christmas spirit like you are doing," Joshua said. He shrugged, holding the string of lights that he was quickly untangling with simple tugs and twists.

Maggie was annoyed at how easy he was making it look when her fingers had nearly gone blue as she tried to do the same thing. She wanted to tell Joshua she wasn't in the Christmas spirit. In fact, she felt as if she had shooed it away like a fly landing on the apple pie at a picnic.

"Oh. Well, this is the block to be on if you want Christmas spirit up to the eyeballs." Maggie raised her eyebrows before tugging at her mittens.

"I can see that. I thought Main Street looked gussied up, but this street makes it look like a cemetery. Except for the Bookish Café. You really outdid yourself with that one, Maggie," Joshua said.

Maggie smiled reluctantly. She was glad the string of white lights only gave off a soft glow so Joshua wouldn't see her cheeks turning red.

"We have lots of Christmas stuff. Your dad kept just about everything he ever bought or received that was wrapped in red or green wrapping paper. It was his favorite holiday. We used to read about things together and..." Maggie stopped herself quickly, before her emotions overcame her. She took the string of untangled lights from Joshua.

"Do you want me to help?" he asked.

She looked up at him with the word "yes" on the tip of her tongue but instead shook her head before the word could fully form. "I'm almost done, and then I've got laundry and some cleaning to do and a few phone calls to make. My sister left me a message yesterday, and I should really call her back," Maggie lied. She had nothing waiting for her inside. Laundry had been done days ago. The house was dusted and vacuumed like it had been every Thursday since she moved in years ago. Angel, her sister, had chatted with Maggie for over an hour this time last week. Maggie had nothing more than a cup of soup and the television waiting for her. She didn't even have an interesting book to keep her distracted.

"Before you go in, maybe we could take a walk down the street and see how Mrs. Donovan's house measures up to the Peacock estate." Joshua bounced his eyebrows. "Maybe make a friendly wager on who might win?"

"I don't gamble" rolled right out of Maggie's mouth without her even being aware.

"I didn't expect you to put up the deed to the house." Joshua chuckled. "A simple bet. Or are you scared you'll lose and have to pay up?"

"Obviously you didn't hear me say how much I had to get done. I don't have time to go strolling down the lane, especially when it's supposed to start snowing tonight," Maggie huffed as she finished stringing the lights along the small nails that stuck out from around her door. Then she picked up the big wreath with red, silver, and green balls nestled inside thick plastic pine needles that had been propped against the step leading into her house.

"We're only supposed to get a dusting of snow," Joshua huffed back.

"That's the most dangerous kind. People don't realize how slick it can get. It's just a dusting. But then they end up in the ditch with three hundred dollars' worth of repairs to their car not to mention the tow bill to get them out. Yeah, just a dusting." Maggie shook her head.

"Wow. Way to kill the mood. And to think I was

feeling all Christmassy and wanted to share it with you. What was I thinking? How can someone who captured the flavor of the season so perfectly with our window treatment be such a Scrooge?" Joshua asked.

"Scrooge?"

"Yes, Scrooge." Joshua smirked. "Let me tell you something, Maggie Bell: it will take more than your bah-humbug to ruin my night."

"If being practical and using a little common sense is bah-humbug, then send in Marley's ghost." Maggie went to hang the wreath on the hook over the window of her door.

"Who?"

"Marley's ghost! The ghost that came to tell Ebenezer Scrooge he'd be visited by the three spirits. Sheesh! Here you are quoting Dickens, and you don't even know the story." Maggie rolled her eyes.

"I knew that. I just forgot." Joshua pinched his eyebrows together as he grinned at Maggie and watched her struggle to reach the hook. She was just an inch too short, and no matter how she stretched on her toes, it just wasn't enough.

"What are you laughing at?" Maggie asked, no longer amused with Joshua's obvious enjoyment at watching her struggle. Before she could slap his hand away, he snatched the wreath from her hand and tenderly hung it on her door.

"I was laughing...at you," he said and took a step back to admire his handiwork. "See you at the bookstore tomorrow. Enjoy your night, Margaret," Joshua teased as he turned and walked back the way he had come.

Maggie was still getting used to Joshua's teasing. He was nothing like his father, Mr. Whitfield, who had been a complete gentleman. How could the owner of a bookstore *not* know who Marley's ghost was? But she was sure Joshua probably knew every line of that movie about the kid wanting the BB gun for Christmas.

"Laughing at me because I'm short. That's original. Like no one has ever pointed that out to me before," she muttered. It was her turn to take a couple steps back and admire her handiwork. The cottage looked nice. It was simply decorated compared to the amusement park that was Mrs. Peacock's yard.

Just as she was about to go in, she heard footsteps crunching on the salt scattered across the sidewalk.

"I just want you to know, Joshua Whitfield, that I take a lot more abuse from you than any other employee at the bookstore and café combined," Maggie said before turning around to find it wasn't Joshua but Mrs. Peacock.

Chapter 2

"**M**aggie, are you leaving those lights that way?" Mrs. Peacock asked. She slowly crunched her way down the sidewalk in her calf-high rubber boots and long down winter coat with fleece around the cuff and hood.

"Hi, Mrs. Peacock. I was going to," Maggie replied.

"I just wanted to make sure, because you will still be responsible for the electric bill of the cottage. You know I'm on a fixed income. And I've saved all year for this so that I could make my house as beautiful as possible. I just hope the money doesn't run out before the holiday season does," Mrs. Peacock replied.

"I always pay my own electric bill, Mrs. Peacock. I didn't think this month would be any different," Maggie said and rubbed her mittened hands together. Her coat was a vintage wool that was warm but not nearly as warm as Mrs. Peacock's. When the wind picked up a little, Maggie felt it. Mrs. Peacock didn't.

"I'm just making sure. There are a lot of unexpected expenses this time of year. I don't want to get caught holding the bag for anyone who didn't plan ahead. You've been a tenant of mine long enough to know I can't afford surprises like that," Mrs. Peacock said.

"You don't have to worry," Maggie replied.

"Famous last words." Mrs. Peacock clicked her tongue. "I have to say, this does look pleasant. Will you have a Christmas tree? In that window, it would look very nice."

"Probably not. That costs a lot of money, and I don't want to spend on…"

"Nonsense. I have an extra tree in my basement." Mrs. Peacock nodded. "I'll get it out and leave it on the back porch for you. Just in case you have visitors for the holiday."

"I don't think I will," Maggie said, looking at

Mrs. Peacock as if she knew something Maggie didn't.

"Aren't they having a Christmas party at the bookstore?"

"Uhm…"

"I know I heard someone talking about it. Who was it? I think it was Mrs. Donovan. She's an avid reader of all things trashy, you know. Anything with a bare-chested male model on the cover, and she's either read it or is about to read it. She told me that there was going to be a party at the bookstore to coincide with the Fair Haven Christmas week festivities," Mrs. Peacock said. Somehow, she knew everything that was going on in town before anyone else. For a woman who was constantly grieving her husband, who had died several years ago and left her a small fortune, she was always one step away from the poorhouse and still managed to know what everyone in town was up to.

"Oh," Maggie sighed. She'd gotten better at social situations since they had been forced on her with Joshua's new policies at the bookstore and acquisition of the café right next door. But if she had her druthers, she'd prefer to just stay home.

"I'll make sure they hang some mistletoe in a

convenient place," Mrs. Peacock teased and winked at Maggie.

"What? Why?"

"So maybe you could finally get the kiss from Joshua Whitfield you so desperately need," Mrs. Peacock said before turning to go back to the house.

"What? That's crazy! Where did you hear that?" Maggie called.

"Didn't need to hear it. I have eyes," Mrs. Peacock shouted over her shoulder. "I'll leave the Christmas tree on the porch. Please pick it up by tomorrow this time. I hate to leave the door unlocked. So much warm air can escape and run up my heating bill. Money doesn't grow on trees, you know."

Maggie was no longer cold since the heat of embarrassment washed over her. Just then, a few snowflakes started to fall as the prediction for flurries came to fruition. But it wasn't Mrs. Peacock's blatant intrusion into Maggie's love life that made her overheat. It was the fact that if that old biddy, who only came into the bookstore once in a blue moon, could see that Maggie had a crush on her boss, what did the people who worked with her every day think?

"This is not what the season of giving should be

like. People giving advice and suggestions all willy-nilly," she muttered while looking down the sidewalk in the direction Joshua had gone.

For a split second, she thought about going to the edge of the street to see if she could still see him walking down the sidewalk, looking at the decorations. But what would he think if she did that? He'd think she liked him, or maybe he'd think she felt bad for snapping at him about Marley's ghost. But she didn't feel bad, because he had called her Scrooge. He'd started it. Then he had the nerve to look at her with those happy, twinkling eyes and the pretty lights making his hair look all festive and his features so rugged. She shook her head as if that might get the image of Joshua out of it, but all it did was give her a headache and make her dizzy. She went inside her house, shut the door, then locked it. She shivered as she threw off her coat, happy the heat was working so well.

Her kitchen was one of her favorite rooms, as it was decorated with the frilliest vintage curtains, potholders, and even a tea cozy. All were in the festive red, white, and green colors of the season. As she looked around, she thought a cup of soup and some hot chocolate were in order.

"Bah humbug, indeed," she muttered as she

smiled at her festive kitchen. But the thought that she could have invited Joshua in for hot cocoa with marshmallows plagued her. They'd worked together for almost a year. He'd been nothing but kind to her, with a sprinkling of compliments and genuine affection at times. But they were overshadowed by his knack for sarcasm and eye rolling, which seemed to surface during every conversation. As Maggie thought of him teasing her, she realized she was smiling.

"Mags, you've got issues." She immediately frowned and set water on the stove to boil. But as much as she didn't want to admit it, she was looking forward to going to work in the morning.

Chapter 3

Friday was busier than usual. There was a nonstop stream of customers throughout the day, buying the latest best sellers from the shelves as gifts and stocking stuffers for their loved ones. Only a couple people searched the aisles, but they came to the counter with their arms full of treasures. Maggie was always happy to see some obscure title be found by a reader who dared steer clear of the best-seller list.

"Hello, Maggie," came two familiar voices.

Maggie looked up from organizing the new Christmas bags and tissue paper to see Mary Jean and Mary Anne. They were ladies in their late seventies who wore their experiences proudly in every wrinkle and crease in their hands and faces.

Maggie had learned through their frequent visits that they had grown up in the same neighborhood and remained friends their entire lives.

"Hi, ladies," Maggie said with a smile. These ladies were good customers. "Looking for anything special?"

"Nope. Just some Christmas presents. We buy books for everyone. Even if they don't read," Mary Jean said.

"Yes. It's our subtle way of telling them they don't have to stay stupid," Mary Anne added, making both ladies burst out in cackles. Everyone looked in their direction. Even Maggie had to chuckle.

"Well, take your time, and let me know if I can help," Maggie said as she pushed her glasses up on her nose.

The café was bustling with the evening rush when Joshua finally made an appearance in the bookstore. Maggie pinched her lips together tightly when she looked at him. Mrs. Peacock's words came back to her almost as if they were being shouted in her ears.

Mistletoe.

I have eyes.

The tree will be on the porch.

"How's business over here?" he asked as if nothing had happened the night before.

"Fine. Lots of sales. Yes. Fine," Maggie stuttered.

"I can't tell you how many people have commented on the display window. I have to admit, I come in here sometimes just to look at it," Joshua said, and his eyes went to the beautiful display of lights and books.

"I'm glad you like it," Maggie said.

With that, Mary Jean and Mary Anne stopped to admire the display too. They pointed to all the books, chatted, and looked at it again, their conversation going on as if they hadn't seen each other in years, when in truth, they'd been in the bookstore just a month ago.

Just as Mary Anne turned to ask Maggie something, the door jingled. When she turned, she saw a short man wearing a suit under a long wool coat. His cheeks and nose were red but not from the cold.

"Merry Christmas!" he shouted, slurring the words so they came out *Murry Chrsms*. When he stepped into the bookstore, he let the door fall closed, hitting the woman who was coming in behind him. She pushed the door open, blinked quickly, then went to the man's side.

"What are we doing in here?" the woman asked in a hushed voice.

"Just looking. Can't I just look?" the man snapped, swaying a little on his feet.

"Well, I'm getting tired, and the temperature is really supposed to drop. We might want to get home before…"

"The temperature isn't going to drop. Just…stop being so negative all the time," he slurred before stomping into the café, leaving the woman standing there by herself.

"Hello, Kylie," Mary Jean said to the woman.

Maggie watched as Kylie looked up. She didn't smile or say hello back. Instead, she walked up to Mary Jean and Mary Anne with a look of desperation on her face. It was as if she was contemplating a prison break. The guards weren't looking. The dogs were on the other side of the yard. The path was clear, but…

"David's had a little too much to drink," she said, forcing a smile. "I think they had a Christmas party tonight. You know, spouses aren't invited to the law firm, so he got a little tipsy."

"Oh, who doesn't at this time of year?" Mary Jean soothed.

"He'll pay for it tomorrow when his head is pounding," Mary Anne added with a smile.

"Are you Christmas shopping?" Kylie asked, looking as if she wanted to melt into the floor.

Maggie looked toward the café and saw David was talking with some younger woman who looked as uncomfortable as Kylie.

"Yes. Actually, that's what we're telling people, but we're just getting out of the house," Mary Jean said. "You should join us sometime."

"Yes, Kylie. We meet here every couple of weeks. You should join us sometime. We only see you at church, and that's usually only for a quick wave hello and good-bye. We'd love to have you," Mary Anne added.

"That sounds lovely. I'd love to get a couple new books to read over the cold months. I'll have to check with David's schedule first. You know how it is with husbands," Kylie said sadly, jerking her thumb toward the café.

She didn't see that David was trying to charm some woman at least ten years younger than him while sipping an apple cider. Maggie wondered if she'd care if she did see it. As she studied Kylie, she couldn't help but notice her coat was vintage, and she wore a pin that Maggie recognized from her own collection of vintage pins. It had a little glass ball dangling from a silver bow. In the glass ball was a mustard seed. Like those bits of amber that entrap an insect or flower, preserving it for eternity, so was the tiny mustard seed in the glass.

Maggie knew what the mustard seed symbolized, and it made her feel sad for this Kylie woman, who seemed nice enough but was obviously carrying a heavy weight on her shoulders. How bad could she be if she liked vintage jewelry and books?

A boom of laughter came from the café. Maggie looked and saw David laughing loudly, his mouth wide and his face red. He was still speaking to the younger woman, who was looking at him and then her watch. Before he could do anything else, she stood from her table, took her tall container of coffee or cider, and left through the café door. David watched her leave. Maggie observed the glazed look in his eyes; he was probably seeing two women walk away. He took a small sip from his cup and headed toward the bookstore. As soon as he appeared in the doorway, Kylie visibly tensed.

"You ladies have a nice night," Kylie said and hurried to his side. "Are you ready to go?"

Maggie watched out of the corner of her eye, as

did Mary Jean and Mary Anne. David instantly got angry.

"No!" he shouted and clicked his tongue, shaking his head before stomping down one of the aisles of books.

"You don't have to yell," Kylie said in a hushed but obviously hurt voice.

"You need to shut your mouth. There isn't any problem as long as you just shut your mouth," he hissed loudly enough for everyone to hear.

Maggie watched as Kylie quietly walked to another part of the bookstore, away from her husband. She secretly wished Kylie had walked out the door, but the woman didn't. Instead, she blindly scanned the titles in the ancient history section, her eyes getting red as she clenched her jaw and blinked back her tears.

"What a jerk," Mary Jean muttered to Mary Anne, who nodded in agreement.

"Do you have any books on French cuisine?" David yelled from the back of the aisle.

Maggie tilted her head to the left and looked at him quizzically. Now he was embarrassing her too. She pointed to the far-right end of the store. "In the cooking section of the aisle across from the wall," Maggie replied.

David clomped over, unaware his jacket hung off one shoulder, his tie dangled around his open collar, and one of his shirttails had come untucked. He looked like he had just woken up from a long nap at a bus station.

It didn't take long for him to find a huge book on French cooking that had been sitting on the shelf for months if not longer. Maggie knew why. In addition to crepes and chocolate mousse, it had crazy recipes for things like cerveaux and couilles de mouton, the parts of animals no one should eat. Only a real chef would want the giant tome, and although David looked like he hadn't missed a meal in decades, Maggie got the feeling he didn't know his way around a kitchen.

With the book tucked under his arm, he waltzed up to the counter. Mary Jean and Mary Anne stepped aside. They spoke in hushed voices as they watched him.

"I'll be cooking every recipe in this book," he bragged.

Maggie wrinkled her nose as the sickly sweet smell of alcohol radiated from him like heat from a feverish body. "That will be seventy-eight dollars and fifteen cents."

David pulled out a wallet that was crammed

with receipts, bits of cash sticking out at odd angles, and more than a dozen credit cards. He pulled them out one at a time, stacking them on the counter before deciding on the one he was going to use for the purchase.

"Seventy-eight dollars?" Kylie asked as she approached the counter. It was obvious from her expression that this was money that could have been better spent on something else.

"Not a word," David snapped, raising his right hand with his index finger pointing up without looking at Kylie.

She slumped and seemed to become visibly smaller in front of Maggie.

Once the transaction was complete, Maggie stuffed the book into a bag and handed it off to David without another word being said.

He snatched up the bag and walked to the door, where he bumped into the doorframe before heading outside, leaving Kylie to chase after him, not unlike their arrival at the bookstore.

"Merry Christmas, Kylie," Mary Jean and Mary Anne called.

Kylie turned around quickly, a smile on her face regardless of the blush of embarrassment on her cheeks.

"Merry Christmas." Kylie waved and left without saying another word.

"Why she stays with him I have no idea," Mary Jean said, shaking her head.

"She could do so much better. She's a pretty girl and smart. Didn't she work at a publishing company before she got married?" Mary Anne asked.

"I think she did," Mary Jean replied.

Maggie listened as the two women talked about how Kylie had been a friendly, outgoing person before she married David Thornson.

"I heard from Willie that David's car is outside Chuck's Tavern almost every weekend from mid-afternoon until closing. You know she isn't there with him. Who would be watching their kid?" Mary Anne asked.

Mary Jean shook her head, her lips pinched together in a disapproving pout. "Now, I heard that he had someone on the side. Someone who works at his law firm. Have you heard anything like that?"

"No," Mary Anne replied. "But it wouldn't surprise me."

Maggie thought it *would* surprise her. Who would want to be with that guy? He was a short, messy, rude person.

"Well, there isn't anything we can do about it." Mary Jean clicked her tongue and picked up another book that she added to the couple that were already in her hands. Their conversation quickly changed to family and who they were buying for. As it turned out, there were more books in each of their hands that they admitted buying for themselves instead of as gifts.

"Hey, we've been good all year, too," Mary Jean said, making Mary Anne laugh loudly.

Maggie thanked them for stopping in and wished them both a merry Christmas.

"We'll be back before the holiday," Mary Anne said. She waved good-bye as they left via the same door David Thornson had tottered through just a few minutes ago.

The shop was busy until closing, and they'd had another successful day, unloading the best sellers as well as making an impressive dent in the more obscure titles. Although Maggie was thrilled by the fact that so many people were buying books, she couldn't help but think of Kylie and the hurt she had seen in the woman's eyes.

You are only seeing a small part of things. Maybe he's a good guy most of the time. Maggie tried to tell herself that, but she didn't think so. Why the relationship between two people she didn't even know stuck in her craw Maggie couldn't understand. But it did. The whole display made Maggie think how lucky she was to be single and alone. It would be a far better thing than dealing with some guy who smelled like the alley outside a liquor store and who wouldn't even hold the door.

If he really was a lawyer like the Marys had said, what was he like to work around? He must have provided Kylie with a big house and car and some form of stability, because those were the only things that could make a woman stay.

Unless she is afraid of him. Maggie's thoughts ran wild with scenarios and hunches. But the brutal truth was that it was none of her business. *If a woman wants to put up with that, then she will. If she doesn't, she'll walk away. People do it all the time, even during the holidays.* But she couldn't help hoping that someday, David Thornson got his clock cleaned and she just happened to be around to see it.

As she shut off the lights and flipped the sign on the door to Closed, she looked out onto the street. She stared for a few minutes and saw David Thornson get behind the wheel of a silver Jaguar. Kylie was saying something as she stood near the back bumper. Maggie cracked the door and heard only a few bits and pieces. But it was obvious what their argument was about.

"Just let me drive, David. That way, you can relax," Kylie said as she stood outside the car.

"Give me the keys and get in, Kylie! Give me the keys!" he shouted from the open car door.

"David, just let me drive," she pleaded.

David let loose a string of obscenities before getting back out of the car. He stomped past Kylie, bumping into her and nearly knocking her to the ground. She recovered, using the hood of the Jaguar to steady herself, before getting behind the wheel. Within seconds, they were gone. Maggie hoped to never see either one of them again.

Chapter 4

It had been a few days since David Thornson had made a scene at the Bookish Café, and Maggie had all but forgotten about him in the hustle and bustle of the busy holiday shopping season. In addition to the pressure of gift buying, Fair Haven was celebrating its annual Ice Fishing Jubilee. TNT Locker Sporting Goods Store and Peak Seekers Outdoor and Adventure Store set their differences aside once a year to combine efforts and throw a party every second weekend in December for hundreds of ice fishermen, local and tourist, to come and not only enjoy Fair Haven but take in the scenery off Hickory Creek, which led to Gracecam Lake. Last year, Fair Haven had welcomed more than ten thousand visitors, and six thousand of them had staked out a piece of real estate on the frozen lake to fish for a week. Half of them would be gone at the end of the week, but a good number of them remained until the thaw.

Maggie was fascinated by the folks who did the fishing. Some just brought lawn chairs, dressed in thick, warm clothes, and braved the elements with nothing more than a pole, a hole, and a thermos of coffee. Then there were the fishermen who would set up what looked like old-fashioned outhouses on the ice, simple shanties that sort of protected against the wind so long as it didn't blow too hard. Inside, they'd have a lawn chair or two, a pole, a hole, and a thermos full of coffee. But then there were the people who would have new-fangled contraptions sponsored by the sporting goods stores. Once, Maggie had seen inflatable igloos that could house from two to ten people. They looked like children's bouncy houses on ice. Tents intended to withstand extreme temperatures could also be spotted from the shore.

Cutting-edge designs on space heaters that would warm a shack but not melt the ice could also be found in some of the shacks. Those were frowned on by the seasoned fishermen. What was the point of ice fishing if you couldn't handle a little cold?

"If you can't run with the big dogs, stay on the porch," Mr. Campbell would growl at the rookies. He'd won several competitions for catching the biggest fish and was reigning champion of the Fair Haven Ice Fishing Jubilee.

Maggie was fascinated by him. He was a gray-haired man with a well-trimmed goatee and eyes as blue and clear as the ice he perched his shanty on. He walked with a purpose and cussed like he was spouting poetry. For most of the year, he kept to himself, but when he made his appearance on the ice, it was as if Elvis had showed up.

This morning, he showed up at the café to have his thermos filled with coffee, and Maggie watched him from the bookstore.

"Good morning," Babs said, flipping her blond curls off her forehead. She'd been hustling behind the counter since six. Casper Lahey, the stock boy who worked between the café and the bookstore, was busy, bustling back and forth between the two. But even he had to stop and give Mr. Campbell a once-over. The man just commanded respect.

He wore a snowsuit that looked like it had been designed during the Carter administration. Thick boots added an extra three inches to his six-foot frame.

"Good morning. You're a new face around here," he grumbled to Babs.

"What do you mean? I've been working here since spring. I know you. You're Mr. Campbell, ice fishing champion of Fair Haven three years running." Babs was flirting.

Maggie watched and nearly choked when she saw the right side of Mr. Campbell's mouth curl into a smirk. That was the closest to a smile she'd ever seen on the man. Every time he had his picture in the *Fair Haven Bugle*, he looked like he had a dozen things he'd rather be doing.

"What's your name?" he asked without trying to talk softly.

"*Mrs.* Babs Whels." She smiled and winked.

That was the thing about Babs. She could talk to anyone. Her full figure was always wrapped in some cute outfit, and the bleached-blond hair and red lips were hard to miss. She knew she stood out just like her husband, Roy, who was as big as an ox and almost always had their newborn son, Earl, strapped safely to his chest.

"Missus, huh?" he grumbled as he let Babs take his thermos and fill it up.

"Any cream or sugar?" she asked.

"Nope." Mr. Campbell pinched his lips together as if he wasn't sure he wanted a married lady pouring the joe in his thermos.

Babs chuckled and handed it back to him filled to the brim.

He paid her, turned, and headed toward the door. A couple of fellows who had come in behind the ice fishing legend gave him a hearty good morning, wishing him luck, to which he nodded but said nothing.

Just before he left, he looked at Maggie and stepped into the bookstore while making sure the lid on his thermos was good and tight.

"What about you?" His voice was low and commanded an answer.

"What about me?" Maggie asked and pushed her glasses up on her nose.

"You married?"

"No, sir." Maggie nearly choked on the air she was breathing.

"Hmm." Mr. Campbell looked around the bookstore, took a deep breath then winked at her. "Smart girl," he replied before leaving.

Maggie watched out the display window as Mr. Campbell strutted down the street. Some father walking with his young kids, all holding fishing poles, looked at the man as he passed and gasped, their eyes wide and their mouths hanging open.

If Maggie pressed her face against the glass, which she did, she could see in the distance the very edge of Gracecam Lake, dotted with the shanties that had sprung up like toadstools overnight. It looked as if people just randomly set down stakes, but there was a pattern to it. Many of the fishermen had the same place every year, and woe to anyone who tried to encroach even an inch on that property. More than one arrest had been made due to things coming to blows because one fisherman infringed on another's territory.

In addition to the ice fishing, there was a dance tomorrow night and sales at all the shops, including the bookstore, and Santa Claus would be making his list and checking it twice in the park for the kids to cap off the weekend.

There was something to do around every corner, and Maggie was finally starting to feel the warm tinglies of the Christmas season. She wished Mr. Whitfield were still alive, but if he had been, there wouldn't be the café or the regular book readers she'd gotten to know. Maggie knew she was not a social butterfly, and if anyone asked, she'd deny it completely, but she'd been lonely, and little by little, that feeling was starting to go away too.

Chapter 5

"I don't think I got a chance to sit down all day," Babs said to Maggie after snapping the deadbolt on the front door of the café into place.

"Funny. I didn't leave the register either," Maggie replied, stretching her arms over her head.

Just then, Joshua came walking up from the back room with a shipment of books that had just arrived. "Babs, are you going to the dance tomorrow?" he asked.

"Does Santa wear a red suit?" she replied. "Roy has already dug out his Christmas tie, and I've got a bright-red dress to match. And we have an elf outfit for baby Earl that has little bells on the feeties and a green stocking cap." Her giggles were contagious.

"What about you?" Joshua said.

"I don't know yet," she lied. Two weeks ago, she'd bought a vintage dress in dark green with a black velvet collar. She had thought about wearing it specifically for the Ice Fishing Jubilee Dance, but as the days got closer and closer, her nerve became lesser and lesser.

"What do you mean you don't know yet?" Babs said. "You have to come. You can't leave me there to talk to Roy the whole time. I love the man, but you and I never get to talk here at work. Oh, please say you'll go."

Maggie smiled and blinked before looking down at the floor.

"She'll be there," Joshua said, instantly snatching the smile from Maggie's lips. "It's in her job description."

"Since when?" Maggie huffed.

"Since right now." Joshua winked. "If you want to keep your job, you'll be at the dance. Casper is going. Babs is going. I'll be there."

"All the more reason to skip it," Maggie huffed back.

"The choice is yours." He smirked.

"You'd let your only employee go during the busiest season this bookstore has ever had? I don't think so," Maggie snapped back. But she was unable to stop herself from smiling, so she shook her head and looked away.

"Maybe Joyce from the bank would be interested in some part-time work," Joshua said.

Maggie snapped her head in his direction with her eyes wide and her mouth hanging open. "Are you kidding? She'd quit her full-time job at the bank if you asked her to work part-time here?" Maggie huffed. "If you want to lose all the business you've gained, then be my guest."

Babs, who had been watching Joshua and Maggie banter like she was watching a tennis game, started laughing and put her hands up. "I can't take this anymore. Maggie, I'll see you at the dance. Joshua, stop teasing that girl and get the job done." She winked at him before waving to Maggie and slipping to the back of the café to leave through the back door.

"What did she mean, 'get the job done'?" Maggie asked.

"Oh, well, I'm not sure. Sometimes I think the peroxide in Babs's hair has affected her thought process," Joshua said.

Maggie was sure that his cheeks had flushed

red, but he was still holding the box of books, so it was possible that was the cause.

"Do you need help with that?" Maggie asked.

Joshua held the box for a moment as if he was really trying to decide if he needed help or not. Finally, he grinned and shook his head. "No. I've got it," he replied.

"All right. I'm leaving. Good night, Joshua," Maggie said. She pulled on her wool coat, tugged a knitted cap on her head and wrapped a four-foot-long scarf around her neck.

"Maggie, would you come to the dance tomorrow?"

He asked so politely and with such a kind look in his eyes that Maggie heard herself say yes before she could convince herself the answer should be no.

"Good. Okay then. See you tomorrow," Joshua said. He hoisted the box up over his right shoulder with renewed energy and walked toward the best-seller shelves, which had become sparse over the past couple of days.

Although Maggie felt as if she'd just agreed to going to prom with the most popular boy in school like in the book *Carrie*, she was confident the town dance wouldn't end the same way.

Once she was outside, the cold air felt good, and

Maggie decided she didn't want to go right home. Instead, she decided a walk down to Gracecam Lake was in order. The familiar sound of Dean Martin singing "Baby, It's Cold Outside" was playing over the speakers along the sidewalk. People on both sides of the street admired the window treatments as well as doing some shopping in the stores that were staying open later. Everyone had bags or boxes or steaming cups of cocoa or cider in their hands. Everyone seemed to be in a good mood as Maggie walked the several blocks past the hub of the downtown area to where she could see the lake.

There were strings of Christmas lights around some of the shanties on the ice. People were walking all over. It reminded Maggie of an anthill, just bustling with activity. All along the edge of the frozen lake were people sitting on park benches or roasting marshmallows over small barbeque pits. A section of the lake had been roped off, and people of all ages were ice skating.

No one seemed to notice Maggie as she casually wove between people, picking up bits of conversations and hearing lots of laughter. She stepped onto the thick ice and walked slowly through the ice fishing camps. The excitement was in the air as the fishermen put the finishing touches on their shanties. The Fair Haven Hunting and Fishing Commission relegated the newbies to the less desirable areas of the lake. That meant they were closer to the shoreline. Those who lived in town or had been attending for decades put in bids and paid their fees at least a year in advance, so it was only fair that they got the better fishing spots. But as with any kind of event that attracted newbies or out-of-towners, someone always had to make waves. The person causing all the hubbub this time was all too familiar.

"I don't really care," David Thornson slurred as he pointed his index finger up at none other than Jim Campbell, who towered over the man.

"Listen, you," Jim said, his sentence peppered with swears. "I've had this section of real estate for the past five years. You either get that shanty to the proper quadrant, or I'll burn it to the ground."

David Thornson was the proverbial fish out of water. He had no idea that Jim Campbell was serious and that he'd probably have a couple of people happy to help him do exactly as he threatened. But that didn't stop David from pushing harder but in the completely wrong direction.

"You touch my shack and I'll sue you for every penny you've got. I'm not moving," David snapped.

"And if you think I'm bluffing, just remember, I'm a lawyer, and I'll drag the court case out so long you'll be bankrupt before they—"

"Ronnie!" Jim shouted. "Ronnie! Tell this guy to get his shanty off my quadrant!"

Maggie hung back as a circle of gawkers started to form.

Ronnie was a guy all bundled up, with a clipboard in one hand and a steaming cup of something in the other. "What's the problem here?" Ronnie asked before taking a sip.

"This guy…" Jim started but was interrupted when David Thornson turned to Ronnie and stepped in front of Jim.

Maggie could see in the glow of the Christmas lights and the campfires burning that Mr. Campbell was enraged. He pinched his lips together and glared at David as the short attorney slurred his argument to Ronnie. He made it clear that he'd paid for this area and that a contract had been signed, and if it was broken, he'd sue everyone involved.

"Jim, I'm afraid we've got a problem here," Ronnie replied.

"Are you kidding me right now?" Jim barked.

"Ronnie, I've had this quadrant for the past five years!" Jim grumbled like a grizzly bear.

"Well, you don't have it now," David said.

"Now you shut up!" Ronnie said to David.

"Ha! It's not your quadrant now! It's mine!" David taunted, making everyone watching shake their heads. He had no idea who he was dealing with.

"Who does he think he is?" a plump woman to Maggie's right whispered to her equally plump friend, who was holding two fishing poles. "David and Kylie have only lived in Fair Haven since the spring. This just isn't right."

"Lawyers. That's a surefire way to ruin any good time," another person muttered to Maggie's left.

Ronnie took Jim by the arm and led him to a quiet spot a few feet from where a tipsy David was doing some kind of jig. He continued to move things around his shanty, intentionally rubbing it in that he had nabbed Jim's spot. He kept shouting that he was following the contract he had signed, and maybe if some people could learn how to read, they might understand the law.

The locals didn't take too kindly to being insulted

by this guy. Maggie scanned the crowd for any sign of Kylie. She'd be mortified if she were here. Maybe she was and was just staying back out of view so as not to be lynched alongside her drunk husband due to his behavior. Maybe she secretly wished her husband would be knocked down a couple pegs. But Maggie didn't see her. She was relieved. If Kylie had been here and seen this, she'd be mortified.

"This ain't right, Ronnie! It just ain't right," Jim barked as he put his hands on his hips and shifted from one foot to the other.

"Just calm down now, Jim. I'll look into it tomorrow, and if I can shift him over, I'll…" Ronnie was not making things better.

"You just make sure you do that, Ronnie. This is bull. You hear me? I paid for my quadrant like I do every year, long before it's due, and paid in full. This is my quadrant. Everyone but this idiot knows it." He jerked his thumb toward David, who dropped his cooler.

"What did you call me?" David stomped up to Jim, who stood his ground and didn't flinch.

There were enough guys watching the whole situation unfold that in just a few seconds, they were between the two men, keeping them from fighting.

Jim Campbell just stood there, but the obscenities flew as he pointed at David.

"You keep talking, counselor! You're just digging yourself in deeper. Believe me. This ain't over." Jim scowled.

"I dare you! Come on! Right now!" David egged him on, his own flurry of obscenities pouring out of his drunk mouth.

Finally, a voice of reason could be heard shouting over both men. Maggie knew exactly who it was.

"All right!" Gary Brookes shouted, his hand on his silver handcuffs as he got between the two men. "What's going on here, Jim? There's kids and families around here."

"I'm well aware of that, Gary, but we've got ourselves a serious situation here, and I'm not going to just step aside because..." Jim said as he calmed down and shook Gary's hand.

"Just remember, Officer, I might not be on a first-name basis with *you*, but I'm sure I am with the judges in this town. Just remember that," David replied, adding nothing but insult to injury.

"Calm down, Mr. Thornson," Gary said, barely looking at the man. "Ronnie, are you sure about the perimeter here? No way we can find some common ground?"

"According to what I've got, this is the spot for Mr. Thornson, but that doesn't mean it's right," Ronnie replied, scratching his chin.

"Oh, it's right," David squawked.

Jim took a step closer to him, his hands clenched.

"That's enough out of you!" Gary barked. "Look, Jim. Ronnie will look into this first thing tomorrow. Right, Ronnie?"

"Absolutely," Ronnie replied, clapping a hand on Jim's shoulder. "You can count on me, Jim. We've known each other a long time."

"Hey! How do I know you aren't going to draw up some fake contract to force me out of the spot that is rightfully mine?" David whined. "You people all stick together and…"

"Mr. Thornson, you have my word. If the space is yours, you'll stay in it. But if it's Mr. Campbell's, and it very well might be, I do not expect there to be any kind of problems from you," Gary said.

David nodded but mumbled something about local yokels and hillbillies sticking together.

"I've heard just about enough out of you," Jim

said. He went to take a swing at David, only to have Gary get in his way.

The men were nose to nose, and Maggie was worried for both of them. This was what David did. He pushed people to their breaking points. Now two people who knew and respected each other were about ready to kill each other.

"Jim! You can't! You just can't!" Gary shouted.

Jim's shoulders slumped, and although he kept clenching and unclenching his jaw, he nodded to Gary. Without saying another word, he strolled calmly to his shed and shut the door behind him. David began to whistle as he continued with his busywork outside his shed just to be obnoxious.

Maggie couldn't help but notice that of all the things he was fussing with, fishing poles weren't among of them. She shook her head and smiled at Gary, who had done a double take, and smiled back.

After he finished talking with Ronnie and a couple of the other fishermen, he sauntered up to her. "Fancy meeting you here," he said.

"I didn't know there was so much at stake at this fishing hole. If you hadn't shown up, I think those guys would have made chum out of each other," Maggie said.

"It seems like everywhere that David Thornson goes, he's got to cause a problem. Nothing worse than a short man with a law degree," Gary replied. "I gotta make my rounds, Mags. I'll stop in and see you tomorrow. I've heard your window is the best one on the strip."

Maggie shrugged and pushed her glasses up on her nose with her mittened hand. By this time, she was ready to go home.

Once inside her house, she pushed aside the evening's drama and focused on a silly romance that took place at Christmastime that she had pulled off the shelf at work. It was an easy read and had a happy ending.

Too bad it wasn't the same for the people on the lake.

Chapter 6

The night the Ice Fishing Jubilee started, the temperature dropped to almost twenty below zero, a record for this time of year in Fair Haven.

Maggie pulled out her real winter coat, which she saved for mornings like this. It was a puffy, unattractive modern coat stuffed with down. The hood made her feel as if she was looking out of a tunnel. Even with the festive rhinestone pin of a Christmas tree fastened to the front, Maggie felt like sausage in casing. But she was warm.

Once again, parking had become a nuisance due to all the visitors. Maggie was forced to park about five blocks away and clomp down the sidewalk in bulky hiking boots that also weren't her style but kept her feet warm and dry. As soon as she unlocked the front door to the bookstore and stepped inside, she let out a sigh of relief.

"Is that you, Maggie?" Joshua asked as he peeked into her hood.

He was looking dashing in a red sweater and black jeans. If he was wearing that to the dance, there wasn't a single woman in town who wasn't going to try to dance with him. Maggie had folded up her dress and shoes and stuffed them in her bag that she always brought to work. No one would know if she chickened out at the last minute.

"Yesh!" she called out from beneath the scarf that was wrapped around the bottom half of her face. She shook off her mittens, but they dangled from her sleeves by a strand of ribbon.

"Aren't those for little kids?" Joshua teased.

"Greatest invention ever," Maggie said as she unzipped the front of her coat. "I haven't lost a pair of mittens in over six years. Can you say the same?"

"No." Joshua chuckled. "We received a double shipment of *Heart and Hearth*, and all the Gooseberry Patch home decorating books arrived. Can you find room for them?"

Maggie nodded as she pulled off her coat, scarf and hat and walked to the back of the bookstore, where Mr. Whitfield had had his desk and hotplate. A single brass hook as old as the bookstore itself had supported her winter coat since she'd first started working there. It was the only thing strong enough to hold all her winter accessories.

"Would you like me to get you a coatrack?" Joshua asked.

Maggie pushed up her glasses. "Why would I want that?"

"So you don't have to go all the way to the back of the store." Joshua shrugged.

"You do know that a coatrack would have to have a bunch of other coats on it to support one like mine. It's heavy and will pull the whole thing over," Maggie said. She walked to the storeroom, where the boxes of inventory were.

Casper muttered good morning before flipping his long bangs out of his eyes.

"Hi, Casper. How's everything going?" Maggie asked.

"Fine. You?"

"Fine, thanks," she replied with a wide smile.

Maggie liked Casper because he was a lot like her: he was quiet and kept to himself unless spoken to. Unlike Maggie, he had a poker face that almost no one could read. Maggie, on the other hand, found herself saying much more than she ever wanted to with facial expressions alone.

She grabbed a stack of books after patting Casper on the back then headed back to the counter, where Joshua was still standing. He watched her until she slammed a book down, turned, and stared at him.

"What?" she demanded.

"Nothing. I just find it strange that you'd turn down a gift," Joshua replied.

"A coatrack is a gift? Joyce from the bank is going to be sad when she finds out your gift-giving skills are sorely lacking," Maggie huffed.

"Is that what you are wearing to the dance tonight?" Joshua changed the subject.

Maggie cleared her throat and stuffed her bag under the counter. "Maybe," she snapped and tugged at the hem of her bulky sweater.

Joshua looked her up and down. "It's not fair to the other girls in town, Maggie. You can wear that and look prettier than any of them will all gussied up."

"Really?" Maggie blinked. She grinned, looked down at her feet, then pushed her glasses up on her nose before peeking up at Joshua.

"Really," he said. "In fact, I was wondering

if…"

Just then, a dark shadow fell across the door. When Maggie turned to look, she saw Gary in his winter police uniform pulling open the door and setting off the bells.

"Hi, Gary," Joshua said. "Keeping the law and order?"

"I'm trying, and I don't think I'm doing all that good a job," he said as he shook Joshua's hand. "Mags, can I talk to you?"

"What's the matter?" Maggie had known Gary since high school. He'd always been a good egg, and she never felt awkward or clumsy around him. But now, the look on his face made her reach out and put her hand on his arm.

"David Thornson was found dead this morning," Gary said. "He froze to death in his ice fishing shanty."

Maggie gasped and covered her mouth as her eyes bugged. She didn't know what to say but could only shake her head.

"My gosh," Joshua replied. "It dropped down below zero last night. How could he not have the means to stay warm? Didn't any of the other fishermen see or hear him?"

"It's not their responsibility to make sure the

other men are prepared for the cold. But I've got a couple of feelers out there to see if any one saw or heard anything strange," Gary said. He pulled his leather gloves off and wiggled his fingers.

"What do you mean if anyone saw or heard anything?" Maggie asked.

"You were there last night. That quarrel between him and Jim Campbell was intense. I've known Jim since before I was a cop. He's a good man but can have a hot head," Gary replied.

"But he can't make a guy freeze to death." Maggie shook her head.

"At the moment, we've got the cause of death being hypothermia. But he's at the coroner's right now. They have to do an autopsy." Gary let out a deep breath.

"You want some coffee, Gary? You look like you might have a touch of hypothermia yourself," Joshua offered.

"That would be great. Thanks, Josh."

Maggie never took her eyes away from Gary, who looked very worried. "What's really the matter? You don't look like you believe it was hypothermia. Is there something going on in Fair Haven that I should know about?"

Gary looked over his shoulder as Joshua walked

into the café then took Maggie by the hand and urged her away from the front door.

"You saw Thornson last night. It was obvious he'd been drinking, right?"

"I thought so," Maggie said.

"But inside his shack was a heater. His car was in the parking lot of the liquor store at Coolidge Avenue. He could have walked there from the lake," Gary said, shaking his head. "It just doesn't add up that he'd stay in his shack and freeze to death."

"But if he were drinking, he wouldn't know he was freezing to death," Maggie said. "Alcohol makes your blood vessels expand so you think the alcohol is keeping you warm when it's actually doing the opposite."

"Yeah, I've heard that too. But that doesn't account for the heater he had and the fact that he could have gone home. He would have had to drink so much he passed out."

"Is that hard to believe?" Maggie asked Gary. "He was in here the other night with his wife, and I almost got light-headed from his breath."

"There wasn't a bottle of any kind in the shed. Not a wine, beer, or whiskey bottle in sight," Gary said.

"Now that is weird," Maggie said. "Maybe he

was going cold turkey, and that's what killed him. Too much of a shock to his system. It can happen."

"Yeah. It's possible. But something just isn't sitting right with me. I wanted to know if you saw or heard anything while you were walking around last night. You had a front-row seat for the whole exchange between Mr. Campbell and David Thornson. Any grumblings that might be of interest?" Gary leaned down a little as if he expected Maggie might have a secret for him.

"Did the paperwork say if the quadrant was Mr. Campbell's or Mr. Thornson's?" Maggie asked, remembering Ronnie was supposed to get it all straightened out this morning.

"That's another thing. Ronnie said he checked and double-checked, and somehow, that little plot went to Thornson. I know that wouldn't have set well with Jim." Gary shook his head.

"Did you tell him?"

"He didn't show up at his shack this morning. No one has seen him. The man is a legend in the ice fishing community. Hasn't missed the event in years. If ever. Now, after an altercation, he doesn't show up. It's a little suspicious, don't you think?" Gary asked then looked up as Joshua came up to him with a steaming cup of black coffee.

"Here you go, Officer Brooks," Joshua said and smiled.

"Thank you. Maggie, I think I've taken up enough of your time, and I…"

Just then, the radio attached to Gary's shoulder went off. Dispatch was requesting he call in.

Before he could say anything, Joshua offered Gary the phone at Mr. Whitfield's old desk. Slowly but surely, that old desk had been getting less and less cluttered as documents and receipts found their way into the appropriate files and folders. The phone was now one of the only things left on it.

"Hi, Gloria. What's up?" Maggie heard Gary ask. She tended to the register and began counting her money for the day. It took just a few seconds for her to realize something else was wrong. She looked at Gary.

"I'll be dipped," he replied. "I'm on my way."

He hung up the phone and gulped down his coffee before pulling his gloves back on.

"What happened?" Joshua asked.

"David Thornson didn't freeze to death. He was shot," Gary said.

Maggie stared at him as he walked out of the bookstore.

"Did I just hear him right? Did he say David Thornson was shot?" Joshua asked.

"That's what he said." Maggie nodded slowly.

The word of the murder spread through Fair Haven like a blustery wind from the North Pole. There was nothing in its way to stop it or even slow it down. By the time noon rolled around, everyone who came into the bookstore and café was murmuring about it.

Maggie recognized some people from the lake last night. She kept quiet as she listened to them opine from the sidelines.

"I'm sure Jim had something to do with it. Maybe he didn't pull the trigger, but he might have had one of his old associates do it," said one woman who had a World's Greatest Grandma sweatshirt on underneath her coat.

"What do you mean 'one of his old associates'?" asked her friend, who had galoshes with yellow ducks on them.

"Everyone knows Jim Campbell used to run with a rough crowd of bikers. Everyone knows that," World's Greatest Grandma replied.

"I didn't know that," Galoshes said. "You don't think he'd kill someone over a fishing hole, do you?"

"You know how men can be over their territory.

If Jim Campbell thought that was his spot, it wouldn't surprise me if he did. The man lives like a recluse. He barely comes out of his cabin during the year, and I've heard that he's got booby traps set up around the perimeter of his house."

"Really? That is a little extreme," Galoshes replied before both ladies left the display by the counter and moved into the café.

Maggie didn't believe it. She didn't know Mr. Campbell any better than those ladies did, but she didn't think that man could have just killed someone over a fishing hole. He was the kind of man whom the slogan "live free or die" seemed to fit perfectly. Killing David Thornson seemed out of character. He might give the pint-sized lawyer a pop in the chops, but shoot him? No. Maggie didn't think so.

But where is he? she wondered. Nothing said "guilty" more than a suspect going missing after the body was found. Still, Maggie's gut told her he was the obvious choice, which made him less likely to be the culprit. But her gut meant nothing. She'd have to wait and see how things started to unfold. Perhaps there would be some interesting discussions at the Ice Fishing Jubilee Dance that night. That was it. Maggie was going for sure.

Chapter 7

The temperature had climbed up to a balmy thirty-two degrees by the time Maggie had locked the door to the bookstore and changed her clothes. She added a sparkly snowflake pin on her collar, slipped into a pair of black pumps, and felt like Cinderella. Thankfully, Babs had left to go home and get ready, and Joshua was helping with some of the lighting at the Moose Lodge, where the dance was taking place, so he had also left the building.

"Wow. Maggie, you look nice," Casper said as he came out from the storeroom, wearing an ugly Christmas sweater that was bright green with a giraffe and a couple of penguins on it.

"You look…festive," Maggie replied.

"Yeah." Casper blushed and pulled the sweater out at the bottom while he looked at it. "My girlfriend has a matching one. I'm meeting her at the dance. Do you need a lift?"

Maggie pushed up her glasses and smiled. "No. Thanks. See you there."

Without another word, Casper left Maggie alone in the bookstore. She looked at the display she'd designed in the window. The lights twinkled, and the star at the top glowed a warm golden color. It was all rigged to a timer that would shut off around midnight. In the window, she could see her own reflection. It was like seeing a completely different person from a different era. June Cleaver would have approved.

Just as Maggie started to walk the five blocks to her car, flurries began to fall and swirl around. It was a perfect temperature for snow. There was no wind and no excuse for the whole town not to be at the Lodge for the event. Maggie was jittery inside not because Joshua was going to be there but because she was interested in hearing what the locals had to say about David Thornson's death.

It took longer to walk to her car than it did to drive to the event. Already, the parking lot was full. People were hurrying in from all directions.

Christmas lights covered the entire entrance. Music could be heard every time the doors opened as people filed in.

Maggie took the first parking spot she could find and hurried to the door before the snow started to come down more heavily. When she walked in, she gasped. It was a winter wonderland inside, complete with a dozen decorated Christmas trees, a roaring fire in the grand fireplace at the end of the banquet room, and a man in a Santa suit, pouring wine. The smell of a dozen different foods made Maggie's stomach grumble. On the dance floor, there were already a couple of geezers who had had a few drinks, showing off their moves.

Maggie took off her coat, and every head turned to look at her. She felt a little embarrassed as she walked to the coat check.

"What a surprise," said Wilma DeForest from the bank. She was wearing a cozy sweater of red and white and a Santa hat with bells hanging from the ball. She was the only teller at the bank that Maggie could tolerate.

"Hi, Wilma," Maggie said as she handed her coat over.

"I didn't expect you to come. You've never been

to the Jubilee Dance before, have you?" she asked in her usual manner, using no internal filter.

"No. But Joshua made it mandatory that I attend," Maggie said. "He said I was fired if I didn't show up."

"Oh," was Wilma's only response.

Maggie took her ticket and walked into the ballroom. She knew some of the people, but no one came up to her to ask how she was or invite her to sit with them. The familiar feeling of her bones wanting to crawl out of her skin started to settle in. With her mouth getting dryer by the second, she walked up to the bar and waited patiently as the bartender dashed back and forth, twirling bottles and tossing glasses.

"What can I get you?" he finally asked. His Santa hat had the name Nick stitched across the white fuzzy part.

"Can I get a Shirley Temple?"

Nick nodded and disappeared down at the end of the bar. Within just a few seconds, he returned with the pink drink and two cherries on top.

"One Kiddie Cocktail," he said with a wink.

Maggie took it with her lips pursed. She hated when the waiters refused to call her drink what *it* was because they didn't know who *Shirley Temple* was. But she was grateful he had gotten it for her quickly and took a long sip. Still, as she looked around, there weren't any townsfolk making their way to her with an invitation to join them. She saw Joyce from the bank in a red dress so tight that if she ate so much as a saltine cracker, it would ruin her silhouette. And if Maggie was going to be catty —and she was—her figure wasn't all that great to begin with.

Is that the way to be in the Christmas spirit, Mags? She snickered to herself. But it didn't take long before the urge to go join the ladies at the bank started to creep in. She was still feeling anxious, and with every passing second, she was sure this idea of attending the dance was a bad one.

"There you are!" a voice boomed from behind her.

Thank goodness it was Babs. She was also wearing a red dress like one of Santa's elves. Unlike Joyce, Babs did have the perfect full figure for it. Roy stood behind her with baby Earl, who was sleeping soundly regardless of all the racket.

"Hi," Maggie said with a huge sigh of relief.

"You look great," Babs said.

"I almost didn't recognize you, Maggie," Roy said. He bounced Earl out of habit more than from any need to soothe him. Like some of the guests would be later tonight, Earl was out cold.

"Thanks." Maggie blushed.

"Honey, I'll get you a plate," Roy said and winked at Maggie.

"Thanks, babe," Babs replied with a big smile.

Babs and Roy were never at a loss for words. If they weren't talking to the people around them, they were talking to each other. Maggie was always amazed at how easily Babs was able to strike up conversations with total strangers at the café. Not only did she chat with anyone and everyone, but she would remember their names or something they said. People were always inviting her and Roy to their houses for barbeques, retirement parties, or other events normally reserved for family. Maggie noticed at least half a dozen people call hello to her in the few minutes after she joined Babs, and another half dozen did the same to Roy. Maggie had lived in Fair Haven for years and could count on one hand how many people she actually knew. Up until just recently, that list had consisted of only Mrs. Peacock and Mr. Whitfield.

Although Maggie liked Babs, she was really hoping to hear some of the town gossip about David Thornson. Since Babs had a way with people and talked to everyone, it was only natural that she'd have picked up some kind of information. But as Maggie sat with her at one of the round banquet tables, she hadn't mentioned anything about it. So Maggie took a deep breath and dove in alone.

"What do you think of the police finding David Thornson?" Maggie asked innocently.

"That was really something. The guy was frozen out there. A popsicle. Plus, shot? What a way to go," Babs said then looked slyly at Maggie. "Who do you think did it?"

The question caught Maggie off guard, making her cough as the cherry grenadine went down the wrong pipe. "What?"

"You read all those mysteries and things. I was just wondering if you had a suspect in mind. I'm certainly not saying that the lawmen here in Fair Haven aren't competent enough to figure this out. I'd just put my money on someone like you," Babs said and gave Maggie a gentle nudge with her elbow.

Maggie blushed again then shrugged. "I don't know. But I don't think it was Mr. Campbell like some people are saying."

"You don't?" Babs asked.

"No," Maggie said, pinching her eyebrows together.

"I don't think he did either. Even if he is missing in action. He's just too cute," Babs said. "Like an old-time cowboy from the movies. I know it's not scientific, but that's my theory. A man that handsome can't be a killer. At least not the kind that bumps off annoying attorneys."

Maggie chuckled. She could have told Babs that Ted Bundy had also been considered very handsome, and that was how he got so many women to trust him. He was also so charming that even the judge at his murder trial liked him. Women at the Richard Ramirez trial had had the guards deliver their underwear to the man while he was in holding. Looks played no part in whether a man was guilty of a killing.

Just then, Roy appeared with two huge plates of food from the buffet.

"Better get up there, Maggie. I think your landlady is about to scarf up all the prime rib," he teased.

"Oh, I will," she replied.

"Go ahead, honey. I'll save your seat," Babs said. She took one of the plates and got a kiss on the head from Roy.

Maggie got up, smoothed out her dress, and took a deep breath before walking across the floor to the huge buffet table. It stretched the entire length of the room. There was an ice sculpture in the middle of Jolly Old St. Nick. Bits of holly and bright-red bows were scattered between serving plates that were covered with all kinds of delights. Roy had been right, too. Mrs. Peacock was staked out at the prime rib table with two plates in her hands piled with beef.

Maggie would eventually work her way toward her landlady and say hello. For the moment, she was holding a warm plate, helping herself to some grilled asparagus, bruschetta, and grilled chicken kabobs as she eavesdropped on the people in front of her.

"He had an argument with that Jim Campbell right before it happened. That sort of narrows down the list of suspects," the woman in front of Maggie said. She was doing an impressive balancing act of holding a brown drink with a cherry in it in one hand and a plate full of food in the other.

"He's a weird one, but I don't know if he'd shoot someone," the man standing with her said. He was wearing a bright-red-and-green tie with the words to "Grandma Got Run Over by a Reindeer" on it.

"You know he was in a biker gang," Miss Balancing Act said with wide eyes.

"I heard that, but that was a long time ago. He's been retired for years and sticks to hunting and fishing. I don't think I've ever exchanged more than ten words with the man," Mr. Ugly Christmas Tie replied.

"Hunting. Of course, a man who hunts would never shoot a *person*." Miss Balancing Act chortled before taking a sip of her drink. Maggie leaned a little closer. "Especially someone who has connections with biker gangs and thinks he owns Gracecam Lake. All you need is one guy with a short fuse and…"

"Yeah, but the guy with the short fuse wasn't Campbell. It was Thornson. I heard that guy would go off the rails just for fun. It might have made him a good lawyer, but it made him a jerk the rest of the time," Ugly Christmas Tie said.

"I don't know about that. All I know is that if I saw Jim Campbell walking toward me on the sidewalk, I'd cross the street," Balancing Act replied before taking another sip of her drink.

Their conversation then shifted to the sweets

table that was just past Mrs. Peacock and the prime rib. They stepped out of line, leaving Maggie holding her plate with a little more information than she'd had when she got there.

Throughout the course of the evening, Maggie managed to hear several conversations that were similar to the one Miss Balancing Act and Mr. Ugly Christmas Tie had had. Jim Campbell was being tried in the court of public opinion. His history of being in a biker gang and his introverted ways were strikes against him. Maggie didn't know if he really had been in a biker gang. He looked like he might have been, but looks could be deceiving. Plus, was that really the way to judge a person?

But the conversation that really interested her was one she heard as she slipped past the table with the women from the Old Cedar Bank sitting at it. Sadly, they did have some inside information on just about everyone in town since they handled every-one's money. But what she heard them say about a certain secretary at David Thornson's law firm was enough to make her stop and listen.

"They were at Rochester's, having drinks after work," one of the tellers said. She was chubby around the cheeks and was wearing a Santa hat.

"No!" another teller gasped. She was an older

lady with braces on her teeth who Maggie intentionally avoided at the bank because she talked…
and talked and talked.

"It's true," the chubby one said. All the while,
Joyce sat there listening, flipping her hair behind
her every couple of minutes. "I'm no expert, but
from the way she was dressed and the way they
were sitting next to each other, I don't think it was
just a casual meeting."

"What makes you say that?" the one with braces
asked.

"For starters, I don't think you wear a dress cut
down to here to go to court," the chubby one said
while pointing to a spot well below her cleavage.
"Plus, she kept putting her hand on his knee or his
arm. Once, she even leaned over and whispered
something in his ear. You just don't act that way
with your boss unless something is going on."

"How do you know this?" Joyce asked as if she
wasn't very interested. She appeared to be looking
all over the banquet room for someone.

"I was there. I saw it with my own eyes. Reba,
you've seen them pull up at the drive-thru a couple
times, haven't you?" the chubby one asked the
woman with the braces.

"I have. I have. But I can't say I saw anything

strange. He is usually just making deposits in the law firm's account. She's in the car with him." Reba shrugged.

"But isn't that a little strange to be driving your secretary around? I don't think I'd like it if my husband was doing that," Chubby Cheeks added.

"Maybe they were on their way to court or something," Reba replied.

"What are you saying? You think his secretary killed him?" Joyce asked before taking a sip of champagne from a tall glass.

"Maybe. But if I had to guess, I think it was his wife," Chubby Cheeks said. "If he was cheating on her, she'd be within her rights. No one would blame her for going off the deep end. It happens all the time."

Maggie thought back to the night she had seen Kylie and David Thornson at the bookstore. Kylie hadn't come across as a woman who would care all that much if her husband stepped out on her. In fact, the poor thing might have welcomed it. Letting her husband be someone else's problem in the romance department might have been exactly what she wanted so she could just live her life in a nice house with a car and enough creature comforts to keep her happy. But Maggie hadn't seen a happy woman that night. Had she seen a killer?

"The police always go to the spouse first. It's in their handbook," Joyce said nonchalantly as if she knew police procedure better than anyone who watched cop shows on television. "Oh, I'll be right back." Joyce nearly tipped over the table as she got up quickly and made a mad dash for the entrance.

Maggie screwed up her nose and pushed up her glasses before she heard Reba chuckle and jerk her thumb over her shoulder.

"I should have known. Joshua Whitfield is in the house. Why she doesn't just ask him out is beyond me. Some guys really just need a push."

Maggie's heart lodged in her throat. Joshua must have gone back home to change, because he walked through the door in a green sweater, black trousers, and boots that still had a little snow on them. He looked wonderful.

Joyce swooped down on him like a hawk on a mouse. It was a gross display; Maggie watched her smile and giggle and do a spin for Joshua, who must have made a comment about her dress. Of course he had. What man wouldn't? She was a bright, gaudy present just waiting to be opened.

Without looking where she was going, Maggie

bumped, staggered, and tripped her way back to her spot with Babs and Roy. Baby Earl had woken up and was an adorable, round little elf who giggled and drooled as he was passed from Mama to Daddy and back again.

"He's so cute." Maggie smiled. It was impossible not to when the little guy looked up with wide blue eyes and chubby cheeks.

"Thank you," Babs said proudly. "He takes after his daddy."

"Aw, thank you, babe," Roy said before leaning down to give Babs a kiss.

"I think Josh is here," Babs said.

"Yeah," Maggie replied while letting Earl take her finger in his little fist and pull it toward his drooling mouth.

"I think they are going to really open up the dance floor in a little while. Are you going to dance?" Babs asked.

Maggie looked at her as if she had just suggested she strip down to her slip and start clucking like a chicken. "I don't think so."

"Would you mind holding on to Earl here for a spell if I want to dance with my woman?" Roy asked while rubbing Babs's cheek.

"Of course. I'd love to." Maggie was happy for

a task that would relieve her from any kind of display of her dance skills or lack thereof.

Babs chuckled and rolled her eyes as she took Roy's hand in hers.

It was just a few minutes before the DJ called for all the partiers to join him on the dance floor. The lights dimmed, the dance music started, and the dance floor was crammed. While holding Earl, Maggie watched Joyce drag Joshua to the dance floor, where she proceeded to gyrate and flip her hair. Joshua didn't seem to be having a terrible time and managed to keep up with a cool, casual step from side to side. Maggie tried not to watch. Joyce was like a fish out of water, flopping around. But every man had his eyes on her. Except maybe Roy, who was twirling Babs around like two kids at a sock hop.

It was easier to focus on the baby in her arms. Little Earl was happy and content to watch the people while gumming Maggie's hand.

A couple songs later, the DJ decided to slow things down with a slow song. Quickly, the dancers paired off and stepped closer to each other. Maggie thought she might just rock back and forth with Earl, but Roy came back to the table.

"Babs needs the ladies' room," he said as he

reached for the baby, who became a wiggling, giggling cherub upon seeing his daddy.

"He's just a doll," Maggie replied before getting tapped on the shoulder. When she turned around, Joshua was standing there.

"Maggie, you look amazing," Joshua said. "I almost didn't recognize you."

"Oh, well, thank you." She blushed as she pushed her glasses up. "You look nice too."

"Funny. I spilled some coffee on my red sweater, so I went home and changed. We look like a couple now," he said.

The words made Maggie swallow hard. *What is wrong with you? He's just being nice. No need to get all flustered like you are about to jump out of a plane*, her conscience said. Maggie smiled and blinked nervously.

"Yeah. We kind of do," she finally replied after clearing her throat.

"Want to dance?" Joshua extended his hand.

"I'm not really a dancer. I don't know how to…"

"It's a slow song. You really don't have to worry," Joshua said as he took Maggie's hand.

All thoughts of David Thornson, Jim Campbell, and some secretary slipped away as he led her to the dance floor. Before she could change her mind, Joshua had one arm around her waist and was holding her right hand in his. Slowly, they rocked to a song that Maggie had never heard before. It wasn't a Christmas song. It wasn't classical music either, so who was singing and how old the tune was she wouldn't even try to guess. She wished she had another Shirley Temple, since not only did her mouth go dry, but she felt flushed and downright hot.

"I haven't dance with anyone since high school," Maggie said. "And I think it was Gary Brookes who I danced with."

"He's a good guy," Joshua said quickly.

Maggie thought it came out a little awkward and looked up at him. He was looking around but finally looked down at her and smiled.

"Yeah," Maggie said.

"I'll bet you were cute in high school," Joshua said.

"Uhm…I think I looked pretty much the same as I do now." Maggie cleared her throat and wrinkled her nose, making Joshua smile.

"So you were cute," he replied.

Maggie gasped.

"Oh my gosh, you're blushing."

"Okay, well, thank you for the dance. I'll see you later and…" Maggie tried to pull away, but Joshua held her tightly.

"Maggie Bell, you need to learn how to take a compliment," Joshua said and continued to dance with her.

Every muscle in Maggie's body had tensed up, but as the song went on and Joshua held her like a gentleman, she felt herself relaxing with each rock back and forth.

"I don't like to blush," she admitted with her lips pinched together.

"But you look so cute when you do it," Joshua teased.

"I don't care what I look like. I don't like that feeling," she said. "Since this is the season of giving, I'm giving you some advice. Don't push me."

"Push you?" Joshua smirked.

"That's right," Maggie replied.

"What are you going to do? Beat me up on the playground?"

"Someone should have a long time ago," Maggie snapped back.

"You are really something else. A guy gives you a compliment and you give him a threat in return."

Joshua pinched his lips together, but the twinkle never left his eye.

It drove Maggie crazy that he could look so cute and annoy her so much all at the same time.

"A compliment is 'Your dress looks nice' or 'Your window display is beautiful.' Not saying things to make someone feel embarrassed," Maggie huffed. She lifted her chin and looked at Joshua through the bottoms of her glasses at the tip of her nose.

"I'm not trying to embarrass you," he said softly.

"Sure." Maggie rolled her eyes. "Well, I know one girl who would love those kinds of comments. She's staring daggers at me now, and good luck getting her to blush. But hey, stranger things have happened." With a nod toward the bar, Maggie saw Joyce fuming as she sipped another glass of champagne.

"Joyce?" Joshua acted surprised as Maggie rolled her eyes again.

"She practically pounced on you the minute you arrived." Maggie chuckled.

"But I don't like her that way," Joshua said.

Maggie swallowed hard. "What way?"

Joshua looked down at her. In his eyes, everything seemed to stop. There was an intenseness there, but it wasn't scary or fake. Maggie's heart pounded like the hooves of a horses on the last turn at the Kentucky Derby.

But as quickly as she'd fallen under his spell, the spell was broken by a ripple of excitement that washed over the entire place. When Maggie and Joshua looked to see where the buzz was coming from, Maggie was shocked to see Kylie Thornson, dressed to the nines, standing in the doorway.

Chapter 8

"Someone doesn't seem so broken up over David Thornson's death," Maggie said.

"Who is that?" Joshua hadn't seen her the night she came into the bookstore.

"His wife," Maggie said.

A couple of people walked up to Kylie Thornson to shake her hand and chat for a moment. Barely a minute had passed before she found herself a seat and had a drink in front of her. It looked strangely familiar to Maggie. Kylie was having a Shirley Temple too.

"Does she know he's dead?" Joshua asked.

Maggie chuckled but then wondered. Perhaps she was used to him being gone for a couple days at a time. Maybe she thought he was away on business or still at Gracecam Lake in his fishing shack.

"She's got to. Gary found the body, and there is no way he would have *not* told her. She's *got* to know," Maggie replied.

"Maybe she's in shock," Joshua added.

"That could be."

Maggie thought back to that day Kylie had been in the bookstore and Mary Jean and Mary Anne spoke to her. She had looked beaten down and nervous, and Maggie had believed it was her intoxicated husband's fault. How many Christmas parties had she gone to at which David had acted the way he had at the bookstore? How many times had she had to make excuses for him? Maybe this was the first time she had been able to go somewhere and just sit and have a nice time. So what if it was just a day after her husband's body had been found?

As if things couldn't get any weirder, a younger man sauntered up to Kylie and took a seat. Then he proceeded to hold her hand and speak softly to her. It appeared that they were admiring the decorations and chatting like two normal people who were on a date.

"Well, maybe she's the kind of person who doesn't cancel an engagement," Joshua said. "There are people out there like that. It might seem weird to us, but she'd be pulling out her hair and scratching at imaginary bugs on her skin if she didn't keep her commitment."

"What are you talking about?"

Joshua shrugged. "I'm just trying to help explain someone's strange behavior."

"*You* trying to explain someone *else's* strange behavior," Maggie scoffed.

"If you want to know what she's doing here, maybe you should just go up and ask her."

Joshua's suggestion was tempting, but Maggie didn't know Kylie well enough to do that.

She was just in the store. Maybe that was a good enough reason to go up and ask her how she's doing. Maybe offer condolences. Maybe just tell her how pretty her dress is, Maggie's conscience tried. But it was no use. There was no reason she should approach the newly widowed woman and inquire why she was at a party the day after her husband's body was found.

Just as she was about to give up, two familiar faces approached Kylie.

"Leave it to a couple of old biddies to stick their

noses in other people's business," Joshua said. He and Maggie watched Mary Jean and Mary Anne walk bravely up to Kylie and her handsome escort.

They hugged her and sat down, taking turns shaking the man's hand and offering what looked to be kind words of comfort to Kylie. The ladies did most of the talking. Kylie looked strangely calm and smiled. Maggie was sure she saw the glint of tears in the woman's eyes as she nodded and swallowed hard before taking a sip of her drink.

It was just a brief visit. The Marys got up from the table, patted Kylie on the shoulder, and shook the man's hand again before heading back to their table, which was positioned almost directly in front of the sweets table.

As soon as they sat back down, Maggie could see the conversation kick up like dust behind an eighteen-wheeler.

"I'll be right back," Maggie said as she began to pull away from Joshua.

"Where are you going? We're in the middle of a dance," he said. He held her a little tighter, interest in the scene taking place quickly fading.

"I need…an eclair," she said and smiled before leaving him standing on the dance floor.

Out of the corner of her eye, she saw a patch of red dash in Joshua's direction. Like the superhero the Flash, Joyce was all too happy to take Maggie's place, and Joshua had no choice but to let her.

Maggie carefully wandered toward the sweets table and where the Marys were sitting. Without thinking, she grabbed a plate and listened.

"I've never seen him before. Do you believe that story that he's a longtime friend?" Mary Jean asked.

"I wish I had friends who looked like him," Mary Anne joked. "But who am I to say how a person should grieve? To be quite honest, if I were Kylie, I'd throw a tickertape parade to celebrate that no-good so-and-so being gone."

"I can't tell you how many times I'd seen them since they moved in, arguing about something. I think this is the first time I ever saw Kylie smile. I mean, genuinely smile," Mary Jean said.

"What about him? David, I mean. Did you ever see him around town? I think I saw him a total of two times, and both times, he ran out without so much as a 'hello' or 'kiss my behind,' leaving Kylie in the lurch. He was just a jerk, Mary Jean," Mary Anne said.

"What's with these girls these days? Didn't she

see what he was like before they got married?" Mary Jean shook her head.

"Maybe she thought it would be easier with someone like him than all alone. Or maybe she thought he'd be different after they were married. Who knows? We don't know what he said to her all these years ago either. Maybe he was a liar," Mary Anne said before resting her chin on the palm of her hand.

"Oh, I'm certain he was a liar. Guys like him always are. There were rumors about him and one of his secretaries. That happens all the time. It's a cliché because it happens so much." Mary Jean rolled her eyes and clicked her tongue.

"You mentioned that the other day. Any idea who it might be?" Mary Anne asked.

"I can't be sure, but I heard that a young woman from Cozy Pines Commons was recently hired there. You know what kind of element Cozy Pines attracts." Mary Jean folded her arms across her stomach.

"Do I. My nephew's last girlfriend came from there. She was about twenty years older than him, and you know he just turned thirty. She dressed like she was going to a rock concert all the time. Yes.

She was a beauty. To say the least." Mary Anne snickered.

"Are they still together?"

"No. She dumped him for a younger man," Mary Anne said, and both Marys laughed. The two women sat there for a moment as pretty Christmas music played and people danced slowly in each other's arms on the dance floor.

Maggie was about to go back to Joshua when the ladies started up again.

"Do you think she did it?" Mary Jean asked.

"Oh, heck yeah. I think she did, and she's out having as much fun as she can before they lock her up," Mary Anne replied, making Mary Jean laugh out loud.

Maggie was shocked that the Marys thought Kylie so scandalous. Yet she was here at a Christmas party merely hours after being told her husband was dead. Murdered.

Just as she was about to go report what she'd heard back to Joshua, she saw Joyce leading him away by the hand.

Normally, Maggie would have been upset to see her chance with him completely blown. Especially since she'd been dancing with him just a few short minutes ago and enjoying every second of it. But this situation with Kylie Thornson had consumed her. Was this normal behavior for someone who had been abused, if not physically, at least mentally or emotionally? Was she some sort of obsessive/compulsive who couldn't miss an appointment without suffering a meltdown? Maggie didn't believe that nonsense for a minute. She was sure that Joshua had just been trying to help, but it was so far-fetched that Maggie wasn't even going to consider it. Or was the answer this simple: Kylie Thornson just didn't care that her husband was dead? Did that mean she'd had something to do with it?

She had that pin with the tiny mustard seed. All you need is faith the size of a mustard seed, Maggie thought. Something inside her said Kylie Thornson hadn't killed her husband, although from what she'd observed, Maggie wouldn't have blamed her if she had.

The party wrapped up around midnight. Although Kylie's appearance did cause quite a stir, the woman didn't stay for very long. She nibbled at a small plate of food that her date had brought to her. But most everyone looked at her as if she was an animal on display at the zoo. If she was there a total of thirty minutes, she stayed a long time.

When she finally stood up to leave, Maggie couldn't help but notice how simple yet elegant her dress was. It was black and flattering without making her look like a hoochie like someone from the bank in her red dress was. Kylie left with her date without anyone really noticing. Perhaps that was what she wanted.

Had anyone hoped to get some scandal from the newly widowed Kylie Thornson, it was quickly forgotten. Joyce had downed one too many glasses of champagne and started singing Christmas songs loudly, off key, making up the words as she went along. She and some of the other ladies from the bank spent a good amount of time luring some of the male guests under the mistletoe.

Santa Claus was posing for pictures, and the buffet tables had been nearly picked clean of food. The bar was still crowded, and everyone looked to be having a great time. No more talk of murder or biker gangs or suspects. It was all "'tis the season" and "ho ho ho."

Maggie, like Kylie, managed to slip out of the festivities unnoticed. Her toes were tired of being pinched in her pumps. She got her coat from the coat check and slipped out the front door.

The snow had really started to come down,

making Maggie stretch out her arms and shuffle across the parking lot as if she was walking a tightrope. Her feet not only ached but were now freezing. Once she made it to her car, yanked the door open, and got it started with the heat cranked all the way up, it took about ten minutes to warm up enough to drive.

While she waited, Maggie watched the people who were finally calling it a night come shambling across the parking lot to their cars. As if she hadn't seen and heard enough, Maggie clicked her tongue as Joyce came wobbling out of the party, her jacket hanging off her shoulder and her purse dangling off her arm. The other women from the bank were not much better except for Wilma, who was trying to corral them toward her minivan.

As Maggie drove slowly home, she considered all the things she'd heard about David Thornson's death. If only Gary had shown up, she would have picked his brain too. But it must have been a busy night for the Fair Haven Police, as he hadn't even made a quick appearance for some food.

Still, everyone seemed to have an opinion, and each one was different. The police had probably already spoken to Kylie. The spouse was always suspected first. But had there been anything to it, she wouldn't have made an appearance at the party.

"Maybe that's why she showed up!" Maggie snapped her fingers. Word of the murder and people playing armchair detective might have already started to put the blame on Kylie as the number-one suspect. She was the spouse. But coming to the party that half the town was attending might have been her subtle way of saying to everyone, "I didn't do it."

As she washed her face and brushed her teeth, Maggie also wondered if bringing a date was a way for Kylie to say that she wasn't alone.

"'Don't feel sorry for me. I won't be alone.' Or maybe that man was an alibi," Maggie said to her reflection in the mirror over her sink with a mouth full of toothpaste. Either way, Maggie was developing respect for Kylie Thornson. These things all made sense, but unfortunately, they could just as easily be flipped to protect her from scrutiny in order to hide her crime.

"I'm back where I started," Maggie muttered then twisted her lips and put her glasses back on.

She wondered what the people at David's law firm thought of this and what the young secretary was doing now that her nights were free.

It took nothing more than a couple deep breaths once her head hit the pillow before Maggie was nearly asleep that night. Only then did she remember that she'd had such a wonderfully awkward and exhilarating dance with Joshua. For a few seconds, she felt the flutter of butterflies before falling asleep.

Chapter 9

When she woke in the morning, Maggie realized the butterflies had morphed into a ball of lead that just sat there in the pit of her stomach. How could she have danced with her boss and let him hold her so closely around the waist? What had she been thinking?

"Now it's going to be weird," she muttered as she swung her legs over the bed. At least there was the comfort in knowing that she had not made the first move. In fact, she had tried not to move at all.

But hadn't he looked so handsome? And he smelled like gingerbread cookies. And his arms felt strong, and that twinkle in his eyes was so hard to forget. Her mind raced.

"Just tell him you had a nice time, and that will be the end of it. Easy-peasy. Besides, you've got bigger things to focus on than that," Maggie told herself as she looked out the window and decided on her clothes for the day.

It was still snowing. The plows had gone through during the night, clearing the street, and Mrs. Peacock always paid someone to come and clear her driveway long before the sun came up.

"I can't have you not be able to go to work because you can't get out of the driveway," she'd said during more than one winter snow. "I rely on your rent to live. I'm on a fixed income, you know. And the cold months can be scary for an older woman like me."

Once she was dressed, bundled in half a dozen layers with her thick, clunky snow boots on, Maggie made it to work. Part of her was happy Joshua had gone out to run errands before they opened. The other part was a little disappointed, but she quickly brushed that aside as her plan to investigate the murder of David Thornson kicked into gear.

"Did you have fun last night?" Babs asked as she got the café together for the Saturday-morning visitors.

"I did," Maggie replied. "Did you see Kylie Thornson when she arrived?"

"Yes," Babs replied with wide eyes. "I was a little shocked, but to be honest, if I was married to that cad and he was no longer in the picture, I'd have been out dancing and singing too."

"Really?" Maggie inquired.

"There were so many rumors around that guy there that had to be some truth to some of them. I never heard a bad word uttered about his wife, but he was a different story," Babs said then rolled her eyes and waved her hand as if to shoo the whole conversation away.

"What did you hear?"

"It isn't right to speak ill of the dead," Babs said as she poured herself a small cup of coffee and leaned on the counter. Twirling her hair, which she had pulled back in a high ponytail, Babs shook her head. "But I heard from more than one person that he was having an affair with one of the secretaries at work. Everyone knew about it. I think his wife even knew about it, but rather than say anything, she just stepped aside."

"That's sad," Maggie muttered.

"Isn't it though? The worst part is that the woman he was stepping out with had been a client of his before he hired her to work at the law firm," Babs said.

"What kind of lawyer was he?" Maggie continued to pry.

"He specialized in criminal law and divorce," Babs said.

"She was getting a divorce, and he was her attorney. I see." Maggie nodded.

"Oh, no. She was accused of criminal stalking and harassment of a woman who she worked with prior to her getting a job at the law firm." Babs chuckled as she spoke.

Maggie just stared.

"That's the same expression I had when I heard it," Babs continued. "But you know men don't always use their brains."

"He hired someone with a criminal record to work at his law office?"

"I guess he won her case for her, so she was found innocent. Maybe the other party dropped the charges. I don't know all the details. All I know is that she was accused of a violent act against someone, and that turned him on, apparently." Babs took a sip of coffee.

"How do you know she actually did this? You know how a town like Fair Haven can be. Is there any chance that the details got a little exaggerated?" Maggie asked.

"It was in the paper," Babs said. "The police blotter."

"Oh," was all Maggie could say. She casually asked for a few more details and was able to gather an approximate date of the alleged crime.

Just as she was about to ask the woman's name, Joshua appeared at the door, knocking with his boot, as his arms were full of bright-red poinsettias. Maggie hurried over, unlocked the door, and held it open.

"Those are beautiful!" Babs exclaimed.

"Well, I couldn't have Maggie's window stealing all the attention. I thought this might liven up the windows in here. I've got a truck load." Joshua smiled. "But I think I have one or two that will look nice in the bookstore."

Maggie pouted then pushed her glasses up on her nose. The words caught in her throat as she thought about how the man standing in front of her now was the same one who had held her tightly last night. If she opened her mouth, she was sure she was going to sound like an idiot, so she opted to say nothing and just look like one.

Back in the bookstore, she let out a deep breath

and shook her head. Joshua came in a couple times to put the rich red flowers on the counter and in the corners of the display window.

Once he was out of the room, Maggie decided she would visit the library on her lunch hour. It was not one of her favorite places to go. Even though her world was books, Maggie was extremely disappointed in the Fair Haven Public Library, as it was nearly impossible to get a copy of any classic title like *The Scarlet Letter* or *Ivanhoe* off the shelves. They had to be special ordered as if they were antiquities in short supply, not classic pieces of literature. But if you needed a copy of some political has-been blathering about her experiences in office, it was not only available but promoted. They knew Maggie all too well at the public library. When she walked in, she was sure she heard a collective sigh from behind the counter.

It didn't faze her in the least. "Good morning, Roberta," Maggie said as she quickly hurried to the counter. Roberta Feedle had been at the Ice Fishing Jubilee Dance. Maggie had seen her briefly as she and her husband talked with the mayor and a couple aldermen. They were employees of the city and didn't hobnob with the riffraff. Roberta had one of those smiles that showed all of her teeth and most of her gums. They had been on full display as she joked and talked with the mayor. But at the library, those puppies stayed behind thin, pinched lips.

"May I help you?" Roberta asked.

"I need to see the *Fair Haven Bugle* for these dates," Maggie said as she handed Roberta a piece of paper.

Roberta looked at the dates and frowned. "That would be on the computer. I'd have to get that set up for you," she said with a sigh.

Maggie looked around the quiet lobby and reading area and smiled pleasantly. "Good thing it isn't rush hour," Maggie said with a smirk as she pushed her glasses up on her nose.

It wasn't that Maggie didn't like the librarians; it was just a fact that she knew more about the books on the shelves than they did. Maggie had also overheard one of the women ask "How do you spell 'backdraft'?" Really? It would have been different if she were asking how to spell something like "onomatopoeia." But "backdraft"?

Maybe Maggie was a bit harsh on them because her knowledge of the classics and obscure titles was so deep. She expected anyone who worked around books to have the same appreciation for them she did. When she had asked how many of the titles Roberta had read, Maggie recoiled when the woman said, "None, but I've watched half the DVDs in the thriller category." When she found out that Roberta had taken the job because her husband was on the board of directors and not due to an insatiable love of books, it made her angry. It wasn't an easy job to work around books if you wanted to do it well.

"Follow me," Roberta said before stepping out from behind the counter.

The other librarian looked at Maggie and then her boss. "Roberta, can you still show me how the collation and numeration files are being down-loaded?" It was the woman who had been stumped by the spelling of "backdraft."

"I have to set up the computer with the back issues of the *Bugle* for this…Maggie. It will have to wait. I'll do this as fast as I can," Roberta said with another sigh.

Maggie was sure this was the first bit of real work Roberta had had to do in weeks. But all the sighing wasn't going to get Maggie to change her mind about looking at those back issues.

Within a few minutes, Maggie was in a small cubicle, with Roberta sitting at a computer and typing in a couple passwords and codes before bringing up the newspapers.

"If you need to move forward or backward, use the arrow keys. If you need to print anything, use the printer icon," Roberta said before standing up and squeezing past Maggie.

"Thank you," Maggie said without concern for whether the woman heard her or not. She wanted to find that police blotter with the name of David Thornson's mistress on it. If the woman was still at the law firm, she just had to see her. Maybe even strike up a conversation with her.

What are you going to do once you get the name? Maggie's thoughts were annoying her. *Go there and ask to talk to her?* "How do you feel about being a home-wrecker, and now that your married boyfriend is dead, will you be moving on to another partner? Did you kill him? You have a history of violent behavior."

Maggie found that the police blotter was almost always on page eight of the small paper. Someone had vandalized a garage door on the city's north side. A woman was arrested for drug possession and intent to sell outside a Hardee's restaurant at one a.m. A man was arrested for public intoxication while walking down the middle of Highway 9. The fact that the people taken into custody had their names and addresses and ages published in these blotters was enough to make Maggie never even think of breaking the law.

After wasting almost all of her lunch hour and getting thoroughly discouraged, Maggie finally found what she was looking for:

Gretchen Armstrong, 24, of the 3700 block of North Ridgeway Avenue, Odell, was arrested around 7:30 p.m. on July 19 and charged with felony stalking and misdemeanor violation of an order of protection in connection with an incident July 12, when Armstrong is alleged to have followed someone who had a restraining order against her around the area of Central Avenue and Maple Street.

Maggie read through the blotters for the rest of the month and didn't find anyone else arrested for stalking. This had to be the person. Gretchen Armstrong. The only sure way to confirm she was the *other woman* was to call David Thornson's law firm and ask for Gretchen Armstrong. Maggie could hardly get out of the library fast enough.

Back at the bookstore, Maggie was swamped. The Christmas shopping season was in full swing, and plenty of people were in town, enjoying the Ice Fishing Jubilee. The ice sculpture contest and homemade craft show were drawing in lots of visitors. Not to mention Maggie's beautiful window treatment seemed to lure the shoppers in by the dozens.

"It was my strategically placed poinsettias," Joshua teased.

"Of course it was." Maggie rolled her eyes without even a smirk, making Joshua laugh as he walked by. Casper followed close behind, carrying boxes of white granulated sugar and paper napkins to the café.

There was no way she was going to get out of there in time to pop in at the late David Thornson's law firm. The place had to be buzzing like a hornet's nest now that one of the partners whose names were on the door had been killed. It was the perfect time to get information, since everyone would be busy answering questions from concerned clients, judges, and other attorneys. Not to mention the fear that maybe whoever had killed David was not after just him but the other lawyers as well. Maggie had no reason to believe any of the others were cads like David, but lawyers didn't always have sparkling reputations.

Still, she hated to be so close to something yet feel it was just out of her grasp. The truth was that she wanted to get a look at this Armstrong woman.

After ringing up the fourth copy of one of

Joshua's best-seller picks, *The Phantom Pilot*, Maggie dialed information and quickly got the number for the law firm. She dialed it while there was a break in the action, cleared her throat, and waited for the switchboard to pick up.

"Law offices," a female voice answered.

Maggie turned her back to the customers perusing the shelves and put her hand over the receiver. Deepening her voice as best she could, she asked for Gretchen Armstrong.

"One moment," the switchboard operator said. Within a few seconds, the phone was ringing. After the forth ring, a woman answered.

"Gretchen Armstrong." Her voice wasn't the sultry, sexy, velvety voice Maggie had thought it might be. In fact, she sounded rather nasal.

"Yes, is this Gretchen Armstrong?" Maggie said, still trying to disguise her voice.

"Yes," she snapped as if she had better things to do than answer her phone.

"I know what you did. Be at the Bookish Café at seven o'clock if you want me to keep my mouth shut," Maggie said.

"What?"

"You heard me. The Bookish Café at seven

o'clock, or everyone will know what you've done," Maggie gurgled before hanging up.

As soon as she turned around, there was a line of people anxiously waiting for her to ring up their purchases. With a twisted smile and a defiant look on her face, Maggie would wait until seven, closing time, to see the mysterious and possibly dangerous Gretchen Armstrong.

Chapter 10

After looking at the clock for the hundredth time, Maggie was convinced it was taking ten hours for the last two to go by. She'd been busy and on her feet the entire time. She had climbed up and down the library ladder enough times to give herself buns of steel, and there were still fifteen minutes until she could shout that it was closing time. Seven o'clock.

So far, no woman had come in alone looking suspicious or anxious, and Maggie was annoyed at that. She was expecting to see some damsel in a full-length fur coat come swooping in as if she had just hopped out of a cab from some Sam Spade story and was preparing to meet the mysterious voice that had tormented her over the phone.

Of course, Maggie had no intention of speaking to the woman. She just wanted to get a look at her. Approaching someone like Gretchen, who had a tendency to stalk people to the point of them needing restraining orders, was dangerous.

Maybe she learned her lesson and turned her life around when she was given a second chance and a decent job at the law office, her conscience argued.

"A chance to wreck a home," Maggie muttered as she flipped the lights on and off a couple times to let the remaining patrons know it was closing time. People hurried to the counter with their purchases, and Maggie rang them up as quickly as possible. Suddenly, the chimes over the door sounded.

"We're closing in a few minutes," Maggie said as she looked up from the register.

The woman who walked in didn't say a word but looked around nervously. She wasn't the romantic bombshell Maggie had been expecting. She was rather plain looking, like a brown paper bag. At first, Maggie was sure this couldn't be Gretchen Armstrong. She was just a customer who had decided to stop in to get out of the elements for a couple minutes. Her expression reminded Maggie of a Chihuahua that was waiting to get picked up by its owner so it could bark and snap, knowing it was really in no danger at all.

Quickly, Maggie rang up the items for the remaining customers. She barely had time to pay attention to what they were buying like she usually did. She saw a copy of *Moby Dick* go past, and she was sure some vintage Dr. Seuss had also found its way out the door. The biographies of Coco Chanel, David Copperfield, and Ronald Reagan also left the shelves. There had been more than five hundred dollars in sales in just the last hour, so Maggie knew more than those titles had been sold. But the suspense was killing her as she watched the door, waiting for a woman who had all the trappings of a homewrecking mistress to come strutting in. Stiletto heels. Red lipstick. Thick, shiny black hair down her back. But the only people moving through that door were the people leaving with their purchases.

Finally, with a sigh, Maggie called out to the remaining stragglers: two twenty-something men talking baseball in the sports aisle, an older man looking in the World War II section, a little girl in the children's section and the plain-paper-bag woman, who was looking around as much as Maggie.

"Grandpa!" the little girl called.

The man in the World War II section slipped his book back onto the shelf and shuffled over to the kids' section. He extended his hand, and the little girl put her book back, too, before putting her hand in his.

"Did you see any good books?" Grandpa asked as they slowly made their way to the door.

"Yeah," she said and went off on an in-depth description of a princess and a frog and Christmas presents and the baby Jesus and a whole host of other things on her mind.

"Is there another level to this bookstore?" the plain-paper-bag woman huffed at Maggie.

"No. This is it. Can I help you find something?" Maggie squinted as if she was looking into the sun.

"No. I was supposed to meet someone here," the woman mumbled as she looked over her shoulder.

Maggie's heart jumped into her throat. Was this really Gretchen Armstrong?

"Oh, a blind date?" Maggie asked innocently.

"Not quite. I think someone was just playing a trick on me," Gretchen said as Maggie studied her face. She ran her French-manicured fingers through her plain brown hair.

"Really?" Maggie swallowed. "You'd think at

this time of year, people would have better things to do."

"Isn't that the truth. As if things aren't bad enough, my fiancé was murdered," Gretchen said, her eyes dry as bones.

"Your fiancé?" Maggie nearly choked. "I'm so sorry. My gosh." This was not turning out the way Maggie had anticipated. She didn't know if she should feel sorry for the woman or laugh at her for being so monumentally naïve. A married man could not be her fiancé whether he was dead or alive.

"Well, he had some strange friends," Gretchen said.

"Really? Do the police know?" Maggie asked, hoping she'd say something noble, that she'd come forward and at least admit that she had told the police about the affair. If David had been lying to her that he was single, that was a dirty way to play too. But no. She had been his client first, right? She had to know he had a family. If she didn't know when he was her attorney, she surely had to have figured it out when she started working at the law firm.

"Someone called me and told me to meet them here. But I don't think they were being serious.

Thanks. Sorry to hold you up," Gretchen said before storming out of the bookstore.

Quickly, Maggie scurried around the counter and snapped the door locked just in case Gretchen pieced it together that Maggie was the one who had called her.

Poe the cat had been lounging in the middle of the window display most of the day but had decided a change of perspective was in order. Now he hopped up onto the counter, his motor running in a steady purr.

Maggie ran her hand over his head and scratched behind his ears. "What do you think of that, Poe? Any suggestions?"

Poe arched his back and pushed his head into Maggie's hand.

What was the possible attraction to David Thornson for either his wife, Kylie, or the other woman, Gretchen?

This chance meeting was not enough to go on. Maggie was going to have to meet Gretchen in another place. A chance meeting, of course. She'd have the perfect excuse to approach her now. But it would require a stakeout. How was she going to find the time with everything being busy with not just the jubilee but the holidays quickly approaching?

"The Ice Fishing Jubilee Dance isn't the only party out there. Death or no death, David Thornson's law office is still in operation. A Christmas party is more than likely scheduled," Maggie said to Poe. It might be hard to find out when it was scheduled, but Maggie had to try.

There was almost always someone working at a law firm after hours. They also usually had answering services too.

After locking up the bookstore and saying goodbye to Babs—who, for the first time ever, looked tired and ready to go home—and Casper, who was meeting his girlfriend again, Maggie strolled in the direction of her car, trying to figure out a way to catch up with Gretchen without looking suspicious.

Parking had remained difficult due to the festivities. Maggie could see her car on the next block, and it was hemmed in by a double-parked car. She felt her blood boil. At this time of year, she'd have thought people would be more considerate of one another. But here was a jerk to reassure her that there was always an exception. Just as she was rehearsing what she was going to say to the person blocking her way out, she caught a glimpse of a familiar face out of the corner of her eye.

Suddenly, like lightning out of the sky, she saw Gretchen sitting at the bar in a tavern called Bully's. Maggie looked around. She had had to park a million miles from the bookstore again and had slipped down a side street to shave off a couple minutes' walk in the cold. The warm, glowing window decorated with spray frost at the corners and tacky tinsel draped across the top was an inviting scene for anyone hurrying by. It looked like a nice enough place. Without a moment's hesitation, Maggie walked in and took a seat at the bar too. There was a man next to her wearing a pinky ring and blue jeans. She gave him an awkward smile before looking to her left to see if Gretchen had noticed her.

Gretchen had taken her coat off, and now Maggie saw what David Thornson and every other man in the joint saw in her. She might not have been the svelte, glamorous vixen from an old movie, but she could have given Dolly Parton a run for her money. It made Maggie chuckle. Men never changed.

It didn't take long for someone to approach Gretchen and offer to buy her a drink. Surprisingly for a woman who had just lost her *fiancé* to *murder*, she accepted.

Maggie looked at Gretchen's left hand but saw no ring there. Would she have taken it off so quickly? Did she even have one, or was it a promise to get engaged that David had given her?

"I've never seen you before. Is this your first time at this bar?" the drink buyer asked.

"I was just walking by and thought I'd stop in," Gretchen said.

Maggie didn't dare look in her direction yet. Instead, she quietly flagged down the bartender and ordered her usual, a Shirley Temple.

"Well, what are you drinking?" the man persisted. He was a tall guy in a suit with his tie loosened and collar open. He pushed a pair of round spectacles up on his nose.

"Vodka martini straight up," Gretchen said, and Maggie was sure she could hear a smile in her voice. The two introduced themselves. His name was Kip or Chip or Skip. Maggie wasn't sure. But she noticed Gretchen straighten her back and pull her hair away from her face. Things were getting interesting.

"One kiddie cocktail," the bartender said with a smirk.

Maggie twisted her mouth as she reached into her pocket for her wallet. She laid her money on the bar, picked up her drink, and took a sip before resuming her eavesdropping.

"Where do you work?" Kip-Chip-Skip asked.

"The law office of Clemmons, Hirsch, and Thornson," Gretchen said before taking a sip of her martini.

"Thornson? David Thornson? The guy who was found dead in his ice fishing shack?" Kip-Chip-Skip asked.

"Yup. He was my boss," Gretchen said. Not her fiancé?

Maggie leaned slightly to her left to listen a little better. The noise of the bar was getting a little louder. The music from the jukebox played a crooner singing "White Christmas," the after-work crowd was chattering and laughing, and the bartenders were calling out to one another in a playful schtick that Maggie could have done without.

"He was your boss? Wow. Does anyone have any idea what happened?" Kip-Chip-Skip asked.

Maggie waited to hear the word "fiancé," but it never came up. Instead, there was another story that just added more knots to this string of lights that Maggie was trying to untangle. The problem was she couldn't find either end to start with.

"There were rumors that he'd crossed some influential people and made them mad. But CHT had all kinds of power hitters as clients. Some of them had cleaner hands than others, but what do I care? I get my paycheck, and that's all that matters to me."

"I'll drink to that," Kip-Chip-Skip said and clinked his glass to hers.

Maggie took a sip of her drink and scooted a little to her left as Kip-Skip-Chip leaned against the bar.

"There were rumors that Thornson and I were a little more than coworkers," Gretchen admitted.

"Really?" Kip-Chip-Skip said.

Maggie thought his reply was a little too anxious for such a delicate statement. In fact, the guy sounded downright into it, making Maggie cringe.

"Yeah. On account of how I look, people always think that," Gretchen admitted.

Maggie peeked to her left and saw that Gretchen had become quite animated as she flipped her hair behind her and shifted in her seat.

"Well, I have to admit that if you were my

secretary, I'd have a very hard time concentrating on my work," Kip-Chip-Skip said.

"I can't help the way God made me," she flirted.

Maggie took umbrage at the woman bringing God into this discussion.

"That you can't. It wouldn't be fair to you." He was eating this up the way a child ate candy. Maggie was shocked.

"No. It wouldn't. So, what do you do? You have a way with people. Let me guess. You're an insurance salesman." Gretchen was obviously used to flirting and knew how to handle it.

Maggie was impressed. The two yakked back and forth in small sentences that were so heavily loaded with innuendo that Maggie felt as if she might be too young to be listening. Kip-Chip-Skip would say something, and Gretchen would titter. Gretchen would say something, and Kip-Chip-Skip would titter. It was like the opposite of a MENSA meeting.

"Can I get you another drink?" he finally asked.

His question lifted the invisible blanket of ick Maggie was suffocating under.

"You sure can. I'm going to use the ladies' room. I'll be right back," Gretchen said.

Maggie watched out of the corner of her eye as Gretchen slid off the barstool and walked behind her to the ladies' room. Not only did Kip-Chip-Skip watch her walk away, but the man in blue jeans and a pinky ring paid extremely close attention as she passed by.

Maggie sipped her Shirley Temple and looked around the bar. All of the people were having a nice time, chatting or watching the televisions placed at either end of the bar. No one was paying attention to her as she sat alone.

After a few minutes, Maggie spotted Gretchen's reflection in the mirror behind the bottles of booze on the other side of the bar. She hunched her shoulders so as not to be noticed. Gretchen didn't pay any attention to her and tittered as she took her seat, scooting it closer to Kip-Chip-Skip.

"I missed you," Kip-Chip-Skip said.

"Oh, really?" Gretchen replied. Maggie was sure she heard a smile that time.

Was this what people really did at bars when they were interested in someone? She thought about some of the great meetings in the classic novels she had read, like Scarlett O'Hara and Rhett Butler in *Gone with the Wind* or Gus and Lorena in *Lonesome Dove*. Heck, even the two-dimensional characters in that horrible *New York Times* best-selling book *Autumn at Dawn* had a better meeting story than these two; they'd met at a department store in the lingerie department. Subtle. *If only they'd talk more about her work*, Maggie thought.

"So how long have you worked at that law firm?" Kip-Chip-Skip asked.

Maggie leaned closer.

"For about eight months," Gretchen replied. "But I don't know if I'm going to stay on there. This whole murder thing has got me spooked."

"You don't think anyone would come after you, do you?" he asked.

"Well, if people thought we were more than working together, they might think I know some-thing. I don't know. Better safe than sorry, I always say," she replied.

"Are you always safe?"

Kip-Chip-Skip's question made Maggie gag. He turned his head slightly to the side, making her quickly clear her throat as if she'd done nothing more than swallow wrong.

"I guess it depends. I like a little adventure." Gretchen returned his volley as if she'd done it a million times before. She was obviously used to getting attention from men. Maggie couldn't begrudge the girl that.

"Yeah? I do too. What is your favorite kind of adventure?"

It was like giggling in church. The harder Maggie tried to control it, the worse it became. She leaned a little closer to hear Gretchen's response. She was sure it would be a doozy.

"The kind you don't talk about in public," Gretchen replied. "If there was anything I learned working in a law firm, it would be that you don't talk about things in public that you wouldn't want your mother knowing. Someone might be listening."

At that moment, Maggie snapped her head in the couple's direction, lost her balance, and grabbed onto Kip-Chip-Skip's arm, tugging him toward her as she swung her legs off the stool to regain her balance. Without spilling a drop of her Shirley Temple, Maggie landed on her feet and stood up straight like an Olympic gymnast who had just launched herself off the uneven bars to a perfect landing on the mat.

"You?" Gretchen said. "What are you doing? Following me?"

"What?" Maggie said as she set her drink down

on the bar.

"Are you following me?"

"Why would you think that unless you are up to something?" Maggie muttered as she adjusted her coat and pushed her glasses up on her nose.

"Do you know this woman?" Kip-Chip-Skip asked Gretchen.

"No. She works at the bookstore I just came from and…"

Maggie couldn't be sure, but she thought she smelled the smoke from Gretchen's thought process as the woman put two and two together. She squinted at Maggie as if to say, *It was you who told me to come to the bookstore.*

"I'm sorry. I lost my balance and…" Maggie adjusted her jacket and felt her pockets for her keys.

Just as she was about to go, Kip-Chip-Skip moved into her way. "You seem to be in a big hurry," he snapped.

Maggie looked up and gave him an awkward smirk. She looked around quickly and saw that quite a few patrons were looking in their direction. After taking a deep breath and squaring her shoulders, Maggie decided to spill her guts.

"I'm not in a hurry at all," she lied. She wanted to get out of there yesterday but wasn't going to let her introverted nature take over. "I'm just going to come right out and ask. Were you having an affair with David Thornson, and did you have anything to do with his murder?"

Kip-Chip-Skip suddenly turned his attention to Gretchen, who stared at Maggie with her mouth hanging open.

"Are you a cop?" Gretchen huffed.

"No," Maggie replied, putting her hands on her hips and looking Gretchen up and down as if she was a hideous piece of modern art.

"Then I don't need to tell you anything. You're nothing more than some creepy stalker looking for attention," Gretchen said, making Maggie burst out laughing.

"Did you really call me a stalker? I suppose you'd know the characteristics of one," Maggie replied without thinking.

Normally, she was never this confrontational. She didn't want to embarrass Gretchen or even make her uncomfortable. She wanted information. But when she saw the way Gretchen narrowed her eyes and clenched her jaw, she was afraid she'd gone one step too far.

"What is that supposed to mean?" Gretchen took a step closer.

Maggie put up her hands. She felt the eyes of several patrons staring and just waiting for a cat fight to break out. More than she wanted the information, Maggie wanted to make sure the gawkers turned away disappointed.

"It means I know a few things. And I'd like to talk to you about them. If you'd be willing." Maggie kept her hands up but didn't lower her eyes at all.

"Stalking?" Kip-Chip-Skip said as he looked Gretchen up and down. Before she could say another word, he grabbed his drink and went back to the table he'd come from.

Maggie felt bad for Gretchen and was going to apologize when the woman took her martini, tossed back what was left in the glass, grabbed her coat, and stomped toward the door. Maggie went after her.

"Gretchen!" Maggie called before hurrying up to the young woman as she slung on her coat. "Gretchen, wait."

Gretchen stopped walking and whirled around, making Maggie slip on the slick sidewalk and nearly lose her balance again.

"You need to quit following me, or I'm going to call the police," Gretchen snapped. She leaned in close and jabbed her finger into Maggie's shoulder.

Her bony digit would have hurt had the padding of Maggie's winter coat not provided a cushion. "If you think you can go digging into someone's background and not get your comeuppance, you've got another think coming. I know where you work too, missy. I won't forget this."

Maggie couldn't find any words. What had she done? Was Gretchen going to stalk her now? Was this a threat? Should she be scared?

What did you think was going to happen? She was accused of felony stalking. That probably isn't a habit easily kicked, her conscience scolded.

As Gretchen marched down the street, Maggie turned and went in the opposite direction, toward her car. There were a few businesses still open for the after-work crowd of shoppers.

But a woman with that kind of temper could have done in her boyfriend. Maybe he did promise to marry her and then broke it off. But she called him her fiancé and then just her boss in the same night just minutes apart. Maggie couldn't figure Gretchen out. One thing she did believe was that if ever there had been a pair of jerks who deserved each other, it was them.

When she got home, she felt she was back to square one. Hopefully, tomorrow would bring some news that would be helpful.

Chapter 11

Maggie had only been in the store a few minutes when the bells jingled over the door and Poe let out a friendly meow. When Maggie looked up, her heart lodged in her throat. Gretchen Armstrong stood in the doorway.

Maggie didn't feel nearly as brave as she had last night. With her arms full of books to be stacked, she carefully approached her visitor.

"Good morning," Maggie muttered. "Can I help you?"

"You look surprised to see me." Gretchen smirked.

"I am," Maggie admitted. "Are you going to beat me up?"

Gretchen blinked as if Maggie had slapped her. "What? No. I should, but no. I want to know what your interest in me really is."

Maggie looked around and pulled Gretchen to a quiet corner of the store. She took a deep breath, smoothed out the front of her vintage plaid skirt, and looked up at least five inches to meet Gretchen's gaze.

"I really don't have an interest in you exactly," Maggie said and shrugged. "But you have to admit that a woman who has an incident of stalking in her past might be considered a prime suspect in a shooting. I'm just spitballing here. Maybe I'm wrong?"

Gretchen pinched her lips together. "Those charges were all dropped, you know. They were dropped because the person saying I did that set me up."

"I'm really not concerned with your previous…" Maggie started.

"In fact, *I* was trying to stay away from *him*. The guy who accused me. He was obsessed with me. He kept showing up where I was. I think he had my phone bugged or something. He always knew where I was. But I'm the one who got charged. I didn't do anything but try to live my life."

"It's really not what I'm interested in." Maggie tried to get the conversation back on track, but that was not easy. Gretchen was determined to be the victim. The only way to get the answers she wanted was for Maggie to go along with the yarn the woman was spinning, no matter how outlandish it sounded.

"I was the one who got hurt. David saw that and..." So she blathered on and on, looking over her shoulder every couple of minutes, until finally, Maggie managed to ask the right question.

"So, you were just in a client–attorney relationship, and then you started to work for him?" Maggie asked.

The whole story was just a puff piece to ensure Gretchen didn't look like the homewrecker she really was. Maggie recalled her conversation the previous evening, and one thing she was sure of was that Gretchen knew exactly what to say and do when it came to the opposite sex.

Finally, Gretchen circled back to the real reason she had come to talk to Maggie. "I was seeing David Thornson. He said he was going to leave his wife, and we'd be together. But then he called it off. He said something about working things out with Kylie and that he had a child with her. You know how men are. As soon as they get tired of you, they suddenly become husband and father of the year."

Maggie *didn't* know how men were. She had had a total of maybe three real dates in her life, and they weren't worth mentioning. One thing she did know was that dating a married man was *never* a good idea. You didn't have to be experienced to know that.

"Did that make you mad?" Maggie asked.

"Of course it did." Gretchen rolled her eyes at Maggie. "He told me right after we…you know… were together. He invited me to that ice shack. Said it would be romantic and fun. All he did was brag about how he screwed some local guy out of his plot of ice and then tell me we couldn't see each other anymore."

"So, you were with him that last night?"

"Yes." Gretchen nodded and again looked at Maggie as if she were surprised at how long it had taken her to connect the dots. "I thought he was going to pop the question. Isn't that stupid? Instead, he's the one who got popped."

"Gretchen, do you have any idea who might have killed him? I'm not trying to scare you, but if you were there with him, you could have been a victim too. You don't know how close you came to getting killed yourself. Heck, the person who did it might have seen you leaving. You could still be in danger."

Gretchen blinked as if she was looking into the sun before she scratched her chin and looked behind her at the door and the display window. Her eyes caught there and lingered for a short time, just like those of everyone who looked at Maggie's display.

"You don't really think anyone would come after me? I don't know anything."

Maggie had seen enough movies to know when someone was acting and when they weren't. Right now, Gretchen was really putting on a show.

"I don't know what a killer would do," Maggie replied.

"I think I'd have an easier time telling you who *didn't* do it. David Thornson wasn't liked by a lot of people. I'm sure the police know. Look, I have to get to work. I just wanted to stop by and…well, I wanted to scare you, but it looks like you scared me," Gretchen said. She pulled her collar up around her throat as if she suddenly felt a chill and had seen people do it in movies to indicate a feeling of vulnerability. Gretchen was a lot of things, but vulnerable wasn't one of them.

"Who didn't like him?" Maggie asked.

"I'm telling you there were a lot of people. If I had to guess who did this to him, I'd look no further than his wife. She had the most reasons to hope something happened to him. Plus he told me before he decided to work things out with her that he was starting to get the feeling she was up to something. I don't know what he could have meant by that. At least, at the time, I didn't," Gretchen said.

Maggie wasn't buying Gretchen's tip. This was a little too convenient, and unfortunately, her past behavior dictated how she had probably responded to David's revelation about going back to his wife. Especially if he had made it in the manner she described. Gretchen didn't come across as a shrinking violet.

"I'm sure the police will be looking into her story too," Maggie replied.

"Well, I hope they arrest her soon. The office Christmas party is this coming Friday. I just have a bad feeling she might show up there," Gretchen added before putting her manicured nails to her throat.

She babbled on for a few more minutes about the restaurant the party would be held at and how everyone had been gushing on and on about

David's death, sure not to say anything around her. She didn't seem to be all that broken up about it. Maggie guessed if the gravy train had pulled out of the station without Gretchen, why would she care if it crashed and burned?

When she finally left the bookstore, Maggie let out a sigh of relief. It had been exhausting listening to her. It was obvious to Maggie that anyone with that much drama in their life had to be creating seventy-five percent of it.

The only thing that had stood out to Maggie in addition to the obvious manicured finger Gretchen was desperately pointing away from herself was that she mentioned that David had bragged about weaseling Mr. Campbell out of his plot of ice. Why would he have felt the need to do that? And why would he have had Gretchen come there as if it was a romantic getaway? Maybe it had been and Maggie was missing something.

She decided a visit to Gracecam Lake might clear things up. As they were, she was sure they couldn't get more convoluted.

Chapter 12

After changing into her warmest clothes and waterproof boots, Maggie managed to drive close enough to Gracecam Lake that the walk wouldn't be too far. Many of the cars that had been there the first night of the event were gone, as loved ones had dropped off their fishermen and headed back to the warmth of their normal houses. Also, the fact that a person had been murdered there might have sent more than a couple of fishermen packing.

With so many layers of clothing on, she was happy to get out of her car and walk the couple of blocks to the lake.

Even though a murder had taken place, it hadn't deterred the hardcore fishermen. Lights flickered behind small squares in the huts that had windows. Smoke rolled silently from the thin metal chimneys. It was quiet, with the occasional hoot of an owl. The only other sound was Maggie's footsteps crunching across the snow.

She stopped and held her breath. From a couple of the shanties, she could hear soft music or voices. The rest were dark and quiet, especially the shack that had been David Thornson's. There was yellow police tape around it. It looked like a million different footprints had been made in front of it. Maggie was no different than the other people who walked past and looked at it with morbid curiosity.

After looking over her shoulder as she inched closer to the front door, Maggie decided she wanted to take a peek inside the shanty. Moving in what felt like slow motion, she reached for the handle, expecting it to be locked. When it easily turned and clicked, her heart jumped, and a wave of sweat broke out underneath her four layers of clothes.

With one last look to make sure no one was around, Maggie quickly pulled the door open just enough to slip inside. It creaked loudly as the spring attached to the top of the door argued against the cold. Maggie held her breath as she stepped inside before pulling the door shut behind her. Still holding her breath, she waited and let her eyes become accustomed to the pitch blackness inside the shanty. Once the sound of near-deafening silence indicated no one else was haunting a dark corner, Maggie let out her breath.

A streetlight off in the distance gave her just enough light to see that the place was simply set up. Instead of a couple of upside-down buckets or milk crates, David had a recliner in front of his hole in the ice. It wasn't unheard of. There was fishing equipment in the corner that, in the faint light, appeared to be brand new. Tags were still dangling from the rods, and the tacklebox still had stickers on it.

A cot stretched across the far wall, and Maggie gasped when she saw it. The shadow of someone curled up on it sent a shock wave of fear through her. Frozen in place, Maggie waited to hear breathing or worse, a scream that she'd trespassed.

But they trespassed too. What were they doing squatting in a crime scene? What kind of sick person would do that? Certainly, someone sicker than me. I was snooping for clues, Maggie thought.

Carefully, Maggie stretched out her arm and grabbed one of the fishing poles. Its handle was so cold she could feel it through her mitten. The long, thin end trembled with her shaking grip. The bobber at the end of the line clanked against the metal hoop holding the line.

With her nerves steeled, she poked at the form on the cot. Nothing. No movement. No grunt. She did it again. Then again. Finally, she slapped the pole all along the hump on the bed, only to feel it hitting a hard surface, not the cushiony texture of a body. There was something on the bed, but it wasn't a person.

Maggie let out her breath again and pressed one hand to her stomach as she put the pole back with the others against the wall. By the faint light from the outside streetlamp, Maggie stepped up to the cot. She probed the mound and could feel a bag that was filled with books and paper. She leaned over and squinted.

The first thing to come into focus was a small plastic lantern. Maggie took hold of it and held it up to the light. It also still had the price tag dangling from the handle. After feeling around the form of the thing, she found the switch and turned it on. It gave off just enough light for Maggie to see. She looked over her shoulder at the tiny square window. It was pitch black outside except for the distant streetlight.

Maggie waved the light over the bag of books. There was a stack of legal pads with chicken-scratch notes scribbled on them. Maggie could make out a few words here and there. It looked like a couple of to-do lists.

The books in the bag were law books and the huge French cookbook he'd bought the other night when he had come in smelling of booze and dragging his humiliated wife behind him. There were pieces of paper sticking out of the top as if he'd marked those pages. Maggie pried open the heavy book at one of the marked pages and saw he'd marked recipes. She was sure he wouldn't be the one cooking them. He'd have pawned it off on his wife and then made a fuss if they didn't turn out well.

Maggie closed the book and looked at the rest of the bag's contents. At the very bottom was a diary—not the kind of diary a young girl might keep but a calendar of dates. The police must have missed it when they were looking in the bag. It wasn't very big and had been covered by the dozen legal pads stacked willy-nilly. Maggie cracked it open and got a glimpse into the daily routine of David Thornson's life.

In the same chicken scratches, he had written

down an event for every day since the beginning of the year. But they weren't for work. If they were, this law firm was handling a lot more than trials and court calls. Seven months ago, on the twelfth of May, David had scribbled in a day at the racetrack, "won eighteen hundred dollars." In June, Kylie was in a car accident. At the end of July, Kylie started another fight with him. It didn't say what about. It just said, "another fight with Kylie."

Maggie flipped back to the beginning of the year and saw that David had documented arguments and fights he'd had with his wife but never listed what they were about. Then, in late August, Maggie started to see dates marked with the initials G.A. "Dinner with G.A." "Spent the night with G.A." "G.A. came to the house." "Boston with G.A." "New York with G.A." In between each meeting with G.A. was an altercation with Kylie.

Maggie was convinced G.A. stood for Gretchen Armstrong. David hadn't been just casually interested in her. He took her places. He spent more than one night with her. Maggie thought of how he had treated his wife that one time she had seen him, and her heart went out to Kylie Thornson. Of course, this was no excuse to kill the man, but

Maggie could understand why Kylie might have seen this as her only escape.

"I haven't caught anything yet. I think all the hubbub this year scared the fish away," a male voice said from outside.

Quickly, Maggie doused the light. She unzipped her jacket, the cold air instantly sending a shiver down her spine, and stuffed the datebook inside before zipping up.

"Yeah. But I can't say I blame Campbell for pitching a fit. The guy had this area for as long as I can remember. Some rookie comes and takes his spot without rhyme or reason. Heck, I'd be fit to be tied too," another man said.

"And you'd think the police would get this place out of here. Look at it with all that yellow tape around it. It's scary and…and…" the first man said, making Maggie drop to one knee.

"And it didn't belong here to begin with and doesn't belong here now," the other man said. "Maybe we should do something about it."

"Like what are you thinking, Stan?"

"I'm thinking we should move this here shanty off the ice, Larry," Stan said.

Maggie gulped.

"This is where Jim's shack should be," Stan

replied. "In fact, I just had a thought. Maybe the fish ain't bitin' because Jim ain't here."

"Well, that is downright profound," Larry replied. "So, what do you think? Should we move this eyesore to the shore?"

"That sounds like part of a poem," Stan added with a chuckle.

"Yep. I'm a poet and didn't even know it," Larry replied.

Maggie wondered if the men were drunk. But she didn't dare make a move until she knew what the fishermen planned on doing.

"I think it's a good idea. We aren't messing with anything inside. We're just getting it off the ice. As a courtesy," Stan said. "You shift that end, and I'll shift this end."

"Do you think we'll need my winch?" Larry asked.

"Naw. I doubt that lawyer anchored the thing properly," Stan replied before starting to laugh. "I wouldn't be surprised if the roof caved in either. If the sucker didn't anchor it right, the chances are pretty good he didn't secure the rafters. A strong wind would probably take her down."

"Would it be considered destruction of property

if the whole thing just happened to fold up on itself?" Larry continued.

The men sounded like boys planning a prank during a high school football game. No one would get hurt, but something was bound to get damaged. And they were alright with that.

"Destruction of property? Act of God? I don't think anyone will care." Stan chuckled. "Come on. Let's see if she'll move."

Maggie clenched her hands and walked across the ice to the door. She waited and prayed that David Thornson had had enough sense to secure the shed to the ice. But the two experienced fishermen had been right. A strong wind would have swept the whole shanty to Oz. It shifted easily. That made Maggie even more fearful of the roof collapsing on top of her. Not only would she be hurt, but how was she going to explain what she was doing inside?

Panic gripped her heart. Her mouth went dry. As Larry and Stan chuckled and began to push and pull the building, the noise was going to do nothing but attract more fishermen. The more there were, the harder her escape was going to be. She had to move now or risk getting hurt and caught. Her body trembled as she reached for the doorknob.

"Give her a good shove, Stan."

"I'm getting it. I'm putting my gloves on."

"We haven't got all night."

"Hold your horses, Larry. This thing ain't going nowhere. What are you in a hurry for?"

"I'm tired of looking at it. Maybe we should just take an ax to it."

"Yeah, maybe once we get it off the ice. Let's have a good old-fashioned bonfire!" Larry laughed.

The wooden box that was the shanty made an awful noise as it scraped the ice just an inch. The walls wavered dangerously.

Maggie couldn't stand it anymore. With total disregard for what she was doing, she yanked the door open. Larry was on one side of the structure and Stan on the other. She leapt out of the shanty, landing on a smooth patch of ice. Her right foot slipped but was quickly replaced by her left. A yelp escaped her lips as she regained her balance and ran off into the trees that skirted the edge of the lake. Within seconds, she disappeared into the shadows.

"What in the world was that?" she heard Larry snap.

"Was that a person?" Stan asked.

"It wasn't a bear," Larry replied.

Maggie didn't stick around to find out how their conversation ended or if they did successfully maneuver the shed to the shore. In her mind, she had escaped discovery with the grace of a doe darting through a field of tall yellow grass.

"Nailed it," she huffed. She looked over her shoulder, confident she wasn't being followed, and skirted the perimeter. With no one on her tail, Maggie hurried back to her car. In reality, her escape had been more like the bumblings of a chimpanzee chasing after a butterfly on a tightrope. But either way, she'd avoided being caught, and that was all that mattered. That and the diary she had stuffed in her jacket.

Chapter 13

Once she was locked safely inside her home, Maggie took a deep breath and let the warmth chase the chills of the entire night out of her bones. It was just a matter of seconds before she had a pot bubbling on the stove, her coat off, a packet of hot cocoa at the ready, and David Thornson's diary on her kitchen table.

As she sat and flipped through the pages, she realized there wasn't anything particularly incriminating in it. It was more like a testament to what kind of man he had been: a jerk.

"Being a jerk isn't against the law," Maggie muttered as she dumped the cocoa powder into a cup in the shape of a snowman. "He might have been a grade-A heel, but that didn't give anyone the right to shoot him."

After adding the hot water to her cocoa and watching the little marshmallows float to the top, Maggie sat back down and continued reading the diary. It was rather boring except for the notes David had made about the fights with his wife. Why would he do that? Who would want to document fights and arguments with the person they were supposed to love?

"Kylie argument. Another Kylie argument. Kylie arguing about money. Kylie arguing about party. Kylie arguing after party. Kylie arguing for birthday. Kylie has a fit. Kylie left the house. Kylie back." That last one was after two days. Maggie shook her head and shut the book. The arguments hadn't occurred every day, but they had happened with enough frequency. Maggie turned to the night when they had been in the bookstore and saw that David had catalogued that as well. It read, "Kylie had fit in bookstore."

Maggie sat back, closed the book, and wrapped her hands around the warm mug of cocoa. "It didn't happen that way. He was the one acting up. I could smell the alcohol."

Scribbled in between the entries about Kylie

were enough appointments with G.A. that Maggie had no doubt there was a full-scale affair going on.

"Wait a minute. What is this?" Maggie's eyes caught a familiar name written in the sixth square of the month of September.

Submission – fishing fees and location. No to J. Campbell.

That was all it said. Had David had an issue going on with Jim Campbell? Maggie scoured the diary for any other mention of his name, but there was nothing. If David had logged every fight he had with his wife, there had to be something that tied him to Jim Campbell. But even when she looked a second time, there was nothing there. It wasn't as if the entire fishing community of Fair Haven hadn't known there was a problem between them after their behavior that night at the lake.

"Heck, the Thornsons were new to Fair Haven. How many other people could David have annoyed to that extent in the six months or so that he lived here?" Maggie huffed.

Suddenly, she felt the urge to wash her hands. It was as if suddenly, the diary might have some kind of cootie on it that could transfer to her and taint everything she touched with a seedy film. There was no point in keeping it. She'd seen everything she needed to see. Now what to do with the book? She could easily toss it in the trash. No one would ever know. But she didn't think that was proper. She'd give it to Kylie. Leave it in her mailbox with a note that it had been found and was just being returned. Nothing more was needed.

She wrapped it in a plastic grocery bag and left it with her purse to remember to take with her. She'd drop it off in Kylie's mailbox before work tomorrow. It should be an easy task. The home address was in the front of the diary along with the name of the law firm in which David was a partner.

"Easy-peasy," she muttered before finishing her hot chocolate and getting ready for bed.

But when she woke up and got ready for work, a ball of anxiety started to roll around in her stomach.

"You're just dropping it in her mailbox. No big deal. People do that, especially at this time of year. No one will think it's weird or suspicious. You could be leaving a fruitcake or offering your condolences." Maggie tried to convince herself she was being skittish for no reason.

Still, as she drove and the flurries of snow whipped around her car as she pulled down the street where the Thornsons lived, she couldn't help noticing how slick her hands were holding the wheel.

When she spotted the house at first, she was surprised. It was a beautiful Cape Cod–style home that looked cozy and inviting. Second, it was decorated with lush green garland and huge, shiny red ornaments hanging from it. Third, Kylie, a young boy, and an older man were out in the driveway, holding what looked like a couple strings of lights. This didn't look like a mourning family.

The older man was not the man Maggie had seen with Kylie at the dance. This man looked a lot older, and from the way the young boy was acting, Maggie guessed he was a grandpa or pop-pop. Either way, there was no way she was going to pull up and drop something in their mailbox now. It was bad enough she'd slowed down and caused them all to look in her direction for a few seconds. Instead, she drove past the house and continued to work.

Of course, parking was a mess, and with the snow starting to get a little heavier, Maggie knew she'd be hoofing it a couple blocks again.

It was a stroke of luck that Maggie managed to find a parking spot just three blocks from work. She wouldn't be late and didn't have to cross through the park. But just as she got out of her car, she saw *him*. The man who had been with Kylie Thornson at the Ice Fishing Jubilee was crossing the street and heading toward an old, condemned building that had had a For Sale sign in front of it for more than a year.

Before Maggie even realized what she was doing, she'd followed him two blocks out of her way and watched him as he walked up the stone stoop and entered the old building.

It was a brownstone that Maggie had admired on more than one occasion for its nostalgic vintage appearance. It had a carved wooden arch over the front double doors, which were now nothing more than plywood planks with the address spray-painted in black across them. The molding around the windows had cement sconces at each corner. It had four stories and four chimney stacks standing proudly from the roof. The brick was dirty, and the windows had long ago been boarded up. The front steps were cracked like uneven teeth.

The place reminded Maggie of an experienced old broad from the Victorian era who knew the secrets of everyone in town, and they all knew she knew. With a little spit and polish, she'd be radiant again.

But for now, Maggie was more interested in

what Kylie Thornson's handsome date was doing going into this old building. She couldn't very well walk in through the front door and ask what was going on. So, with her bulky purse holding David Thornson's diary slung over her shoulder, Maggie casually strolled closer to the grand old building. Before anyone could notice, she turned and headed innocently down the gangway following along the side of the building. A rusted chain-link fence ran along the edge of the sidewalk. In the summer, it was covered in viny weeds, but now, nothing more than the dried, thin remains of dead plants wove through the links, leaving the back of the property in full view. At one corner, it was bent up, indicating that Maggie wouldn't be the first and probably not the last person to trespass on the property.

With a quick glance around, she pulled the fence back and slipped underneath, careful to duck so her knit cap wouldn't get snagged. Once inside the fence, Maggie walked up to the building. The back door was a plank of plywood bearing the words NO TRESPASSING in the same black spray paint as the front door. The windows were criss-crossed with boards.

As Maggie made her way carefully across the yard, the snow crunching under her boots, she studied the windows, looking for a spot to peek in. Just off the back door was a window that had a couple boards missing. Obviously, people had gotten inside this way. Careful not to slip on the cracked back steps, Maggie crept up to the opening. With her hands cupped over her eyes, she peered inside. It was almost black except for the shafts of light that cut through the dusty air from the windows. It was quiet for a moment, but then Maggie heard a woman's voice.

"Is that you?"

"Yes, it is," the mystery man replied.

Maggie heard footsteps and squinted between the slats. The smell of dust and mold wafted through the opening.

"Has there been any news?" the woman asked.

"Not a peep. No one knows a thing. No one *suspects* a thing. I think you are good to go. I'm the deciding factor, right?"

"And?" the woman said.

"And the answer is yes," he replied.

"Really?"

"Really, Kylie. The answer is a resounding yes," he said, the smile coming through in his voice.

Maggie shifted, standing on her tiptoes to see

into the darkness. As if she were watching a movie, she saw the two people embrace.

"Oh my gosh!" Kylie gasped, overcome with emotion.

Maggie didn't think she'd asked the man to marry her. What kind of a woman would do that?

"It's going to be all right now," the man said.

Maggie hadn't heard Kylie mention his name. Who the heck was he?

"You deserve this. After all you've been through. You deserve this, and I'm telling you now that…"

"Hey! Hey, you!" Maggie heard from behind her. Without thinking about the ice and snow, Maggie pulled back from the window and whirled around. In the gangway, a large man wearing a Green Bay Packers knit cap pointed a thick finger at her.

"Uh…uh…" Maggie took a careful step away from the window. Her mind whipped like a gust of wind caught in a corner between two buildings.

"That's private property! Get away from there!" he shouted as he scanned the fence for the point of entry. Once he saw it, he darted for it, pulling the fence back as if it was made of nothing more than aluminum foil.

Maggie's eyes bulged. Without thinking, she

dashed down the steps and ran around the other side of the building, hoping there would be a way out. There was: up and over the fence.

Maggie couldn't recall the last time she had scaled a chain-link fence, if she ever had. Most of her younger years had been spent with her nose in her books. But she was sure the man in the Green Bay cap was charging right behind her like a rhinoceros. Climbing a fence was suddenly the greatest idea she'd ever had. There was only one way out of this unless she wanted to be charged with trespassing, spying, and who knew what else they could say she did.

As she threw herself into the fence, she wedged the toe of one boot into a link and then the other. With all her strength, she grabbed as high on the links as she could and pulled herself up. Before she knew it, one leg was over the top. There she was, on top of the fence with her bulky boots dangling on either side. It looked very high to just jump to the ground.

"What are you doing, Margaret Bell? You're insane. Climbing fences and jumping from dizzying heights." She scowled and looked back in the direction of the Green Bay man. She was sure it was his huffing and puffing she heard closing in.

Before almost losing her balance astride the fence, she swung her left leg over. It was impossible to wedge her boot into the links from this angle. With the metal points digging into her backside, Maggie took a deep breath and held it as if she were jumping into the deep end of a pool.

Her eyes nearly popped out of her head, her arms went up in the air, and when she landed, gravity pulled her over to the side as her boots sank about six inches into the drifted snow. There was no time to lose. She got to her feet and took off in the direction of the bookstore. No one in a green-and-yellow Green Bay cap came lumbering after her. No one from inside the house came to look and point in her direction. She'd escaped for the second time in twenty-four hours.

As she gasped for air after finally slowing her pace, Maggie shook her head.

"What are you thinking? You can't keep doing things like this. This is totally out of character for you. One of these days, you are going to break your neck, and then what?" she muttered. The morning pedestrians walked past, giving her the same amount of space that they'd give a transient with smelly clothes and a dirty face who mumbled to herself.

Once she was inside the bookstore, the smell of freshly brewed coffee and the sight of books neatly arranged on the shelves, along with Poe's pleasant purring as he stretched out on the counter, waiting for Maggie to scratch behind his ears, had a calming effect.

"Good morning, kitty," she said as she lowered her head toward Poe. He gave her an affectionate head butt.

Once out of her coat and scarf, Maggie opened the bookstore for business. People immediately wandered over from the café. Books of all kinds were sold, making Maggie very happy. She found herself chatting pleasantly with some of the customers, wishing everyone a merry Christmas as they left, whether they bought something or not. But behind the pleasantries, she couldn't stop herself from trying to figure out what Kylie and her mystery man had been doing in that abandoned building, and what had they meant when they spoke of no one knowing anything?

"It has to have something to do with David's death. It can't mean any other thing, can it?" she muttered as she straightened up the counter.

The conversation she carried out with herself caused several patrons to stop and stare at her.

When she realized she had an audience, her cheeks flushed. She pushed up her glasses. No smart remarks or excuses came to mind, so she just busied herself with stacking bags and tissue paper.

The question now was how Maggie was going to find out anything about Kylie. She didn't know the woman at all. From what she'd seen and heard on that night she had been in the bookstore, even the Marys didn't know that much about her except what they'd heard.

"Even if they did know her well, how would I go about getting information from her? I don't know Kylie. I certainly don't know her dead husband. I can't go offer my condolences without looking like a complete weirdo," she muttered.

"You? Look like a complete weirdo? Who said that?" Joshua teased as he walked past with Casper following close behind.

"No one said that. That's what I'm *saying*," Maggie huffed with her eyebrows pinched together.

Joshua and Casper started to laugh.

"I certainly don't see what is so funny."

"Do you see what's so funny?" Joshua asked Casper.

"Maggie just makes me laugh," Casper said

with a smile in Maggie's direction. "I don't mean anything by it, Maggie."

Pulling her lips down at the corners, she stared at Joshua and Casper, making them laugh even more before they made their way to the café. As much as she wanted to pretend to be mad, she just couldn't. Even though Casper was as quiet as a church mouse and Joshua was as loud as a steam locomotive, Maggie was crazy about them both. To think that she had felt such anger at Joshua just a short while ago for changing things at the bookshop. It was a true miracle that she'd come to feel the way she did for him now.

You have such a crush on him, her conscience needled. She shook her head as the internal debate continued.

I can appreciate our differences. Together, we have managed to make the bookshop a real success. That's all, she mused.

But you think he's good-looking.

Of course he is. But a man has to be more than that to be someone special. She nodded as if she had just made the most brilliant move in her internal chess game.

And even though you have been trying to forget it, you felt a little more than just friendship when he held you close at the dance.

Maggie had been trying to forget that. She'd desperately and intentionally kept it out of her mind and focused on anything but those few precious moments that had made her tingle all over.

I'm still not going to think about that. It's obvious that he was just being nice. I'm his employee. He made me go to the dance, and so he had to make a special effort in order to make me feel I hadn't wasted my time. That's all.

He sure did hold you close. That little voice was suddenly determined to make Maggie a blushing, stuttering mess.

It was nothing, and I don't want to think about it anymore, Maggie said unaware that her lips were moving and she was blinking as if she'd accidentally looked into a flashlight.

"Who are you talking to?" Joshua asked as he walked past.

"What?" Maggie jumped.

"Are you talking to me?"

"Eww. No," she snapped, her face in a grimace as she tried and failed not to be embarrassed.

Joshua looked at her with a sly smile as he approached the counter. "Did you just say *eww?*"

"Yes," Maggie replied, wishing someone,

anyone would come up to the counter with a purchase. Alas, she was alone with nothing but the counter separating her from Joshua.

"Well, that's what I deserve, I guess. Maybe I haven't told you enough how well you are doing. I've had more than one customer come up and tell me what a pleasure it is to deal with you and that you are very knowledgeable about seventy-five percent of the books and…"

"Only seventy-five percent?" Maggie frowned.

"Maggie, that's amazing. I don't think…"

"I'm sure that I know more than that about the books on the shelves. I've read most of them. With the exception of a couple on mathematical theories and the history of rugby, I'd say I know a good bit more than seventy-five percent." Maggie put her hands on her hips.

"I'm trying to give you a compliment," Joshua nagged.

"By telling me I barely know anything about the books on the shelves?"

"I didn't even say that! Maggie Bell, you are impossible to please!"

"Maybe so, Joshua Whitfield, but you don't know your percentages, because I'm topping off at eighty-eight, maybe more like eighty-nine percent knowledge on all the titles here!" Maggie waved her hand around as if she was showcasing a new car on a game show.

"Are you done?"

"Even those so-called best sellers that you like so much," Maggie said as she pointed to the books framing the door that joined the café to the bookstore.

"Is that all?" Joshua snapped.

"No. It wouldn't hurt you to read something other than *Sports Illustrated* or *Consumer Reports*. A lot can be learned from the books on these shelves. I should know. I've read most of them," Maggie huffed before folding her arms over her chest, her breath coming a little more heavily than normal.

Joshua stood there for a moment before he burst out laughing, making Maggie even more annoyed.

"I don't read either one of those magazines," he taunted. "But I will tell you this. For someone who has read almost everything on these shelves, including the romance section, you can't convince me you learned a thing."

Maggie's mouth fell open as she watched Joshua walk backward, smirking at her, before disappearing into the small kitchen area he was slowly converting into an actual office.

"Miss?" An older man interrupted her thoughts with three paperbacks in one hand and his wallet in the other.

"I'm sorry, sir," Maggie said. "My boss has yet to learn how to use his indoor voice."

"Maybe he likes you," the older man said with a stoic look on his face as if he'd been studying the whole exchange.

Maggie looked at him as if he had suddenly sprouted a third eye in the middle of his forehead. Not a single retort or comeback came to mind. Instead, she rang up his purchase and wished him a merry Christmas with an embarrassed smile.

The man chuckled as he wished her the same and left, leaving only the jingle of the bells over the door in his wake.

Chapter 14

Once Maggie had finally straightened up the store and locked it up for the night, she didn't know what to do about Kylie Thornson or her mystery man or the date book she was carrying around that was Kylie's dead husband's. But then genius struck.

As Maggie was walking to her car, careful to avoid any connection with the condemned brownstone, she saw two women with clipboards walking in her direction. They were admiring all the decorations in the store windows and the festive ornaments hanging from the light poles while marking something on the sheets of paper clipped to those boards.

She quickly turned around and went back to the bookstore for a clipboard and some random pieces of paper. It was a little tricky finding the house in the dark, but finally, Maggie managed to retrace her steps from that morning and found the Thornson residence. It had been decorated simply with a couple strings of red, white, and green lights. There was a Christmas tree twinkling in the front bay window.

After parking her car on the street, Maggie walked down the sidewalk to the house. For just a few seconds, she contemplated turning and running, but she'd already done some running today and decided she didn't want to do anymore. Without giving herself the opportunity to talk herself out of it, she rang the doorbell. Within seconds, Kylie Thornson answered the door.

"Hi," Maggie said and cleared her throat. "My name is Maggie Bell. I'm helping with the Neighborhood Decorating Committee and wanted to know if I could ask you a few questions about the houses on your block that are participating in the contest." Maggie waited for the door to be shut in her face. What kind of a harebrained idea was this? A woman in mourning wasn't going to want to talk about anything, especially with a stranger.

"Of course. Come on in, Maggie. I'm Kylie Thornson," she said. She held the door open and stepped aside, letting Maggie in.

"Thanks," Maggie said as her blood pressure spiked. She hadn't really prepared anything, since she had been sure this was going to be a dead end. "The weather has been pretty accommodating so far. That's why we are gathering information now, just in case Mother Nature decides to throw us a curveball."

"Good idea. Would you like a glass of water or a hot chocolate or something?" Kylie was as pleasant in her home as she had been in the bookstore.

As Maggie looked around, she saw lots of pictures of a little boy who had the same hair and eyes as Kylie. The house was neat but still had that lived-in look about it. There were some toys on the steps leading upstairs. There were a couple dishes in the sink. A pile of dust in front of a broom that had been propped in a corner waited for a dustpan and a couple swipes. The curtains over the windows were simple lace valances. The theme was grapes. There was nothing around to indicate there was any trouble or that a death had disrupted anything.

"A glass of water would be fine," Maggie

replied. "What a lovely kitchen." She hated small talk. Nothing brought a conversation to a halt like mindless blather about nothing important. The kitchen was small, with a breakfast nook by a set of three windows. There was a back door where coats and boots were carefully placed on their proper pegs and mats.

"Thank you. So, what can I answer for you?" Kylie asked cheerfully as she got a glass down from the cupboard and filled it from the tap.

"Yes. First, will you be participating in the home-decorating competition? They insist we call it a competition instead of a contest," Maggie fibbed.

"No," Kylie replied before setting the glass of water on the kitchen table in front of Maggie. "We've had some bad news here. My husband passed away, and so things are going to be a little quiet this holiday."

Maggie watched Kylie carefully. "I'm so sorry. Had he been ill for a while?"

"I guess that depends on your definition of ill," Kylie muttered. "Actually, he was shot. The police are looking into it."

The words just ran off Kylie's tongue as if she had been repeating the same line for years. Like someone who was reciting their favorite quote from a movie.

"I'm so sorry," Maggie replied sincerely.

"Thank you. What else did you need to know for the decorating committee?" Kylie smiled pleasantly.

She was prettier than Maggie had remembered. But the weight of an intoxicated husband was bound to make a woman look a little out of shape. It was obvious that Kylie wasn't going to share too many details about her late husband. Thinking quickly, Maggie continued her line of questions.

"Do you have a favorite house on your block that is decorated that you'd like to nominate for the competition?" Maggie looked at the paper on her clipboard, which held nothing but an invoice from three months ago listing twenty copies of *One to Cover It Up* and six replacement copies of *The Ferret in the Attic* that had been damaged in the first shipment.

"You know, it may not be the fanciest house on the block, but about four doors down, there is a house I think looks precious. That family has four children and I think one more on the way. They are really celebrating the season, and I think the kids are the ones that decorated the house. They would get such a kick out of it if they got some kind of award or even a mention in the paper," Kylie gushed.

Suddenly, Maggie felt terrible for the lie she was perpetrating. "That's really nice of you to say so." Maggie cleared her throat. The guilt was overwhelming.

Just then, the man Maggie had seen in the driveway appeared in the kitchen doorway.

"Dad, this is Maggie Bell. She's with the House Decorating Committee. This is my father, Anthony," Kylie said politely.

"Hello," the man said, smiling pleasantly.

"Hi," Maggie replied. "Uhm, Kylie told me about your loss. I'm so sorry."

"It wasn't much of a loss," Anthony replied with a bitter chuckle.

"Dad." Kylie took a deep breath. She didn't seem upset at her father's comment. But she did seem tired of it, as if she'd heard it enough times already.

"Then…congratulations?" Maggie raised her eyebrows innocently.

"I'm seventy years old. I don't have to watch

what I say," Anthony replied, making Kylie roll her eyes.

"My father didn't like my husband," Kylie admitted. "The only reason the police haven't locked him in the pokey for the crime is because we were all together the night David was…" She swallowed and shrugged.

"He was a no-good so-and-so," Anthony huffed. He went to the refrigerator and grabbed himself a bottle of water. "If I were just ten years younger, I would have handled him myself, and I don't care who knows it. He was no good. And I don't care who knows that either."

A lot of people know it, Maggie thought.

"Okay, Dad. I think we all get the picture," Kylie said.

"I don't know who did him in, but I'm *not* ashamed to say I'd shake his hand. That man is a friend of mine. For what David put my daughter through, he got off easy," Anthony continued.

"Dad? Did you put Leo to bed?" Kylie asked.

"Yeah. He wanted to read for a little while, so I told him he could," Anthony replied. "Leo is my grandson." Anthony's eyes began to twinkle at the mere mention of the boy Maggie had seen outside that morning.

"How old is he?" Maggie asked, guessing maybe six or seven.

"He's seven," Anthony replied proudly.

"How is he taking the news?" Maggie asked boldly.

"Ha! He doesn't seem to mind," Anthony replied.

"Dad? He's a little boy. I don't think it has sunk in yet," Kylie replied.

But Maggie didn't think Kylie really believed her own words. From the looks of things, everyone in the family seemed to be sort of, kind of okay with the murder.

"Little boys are usually closest with their dads. At least, that's what I've heard. I don't have any kids," Maggie gently probed.

"He's closest with Grandpa. David was always too busy to be a dad. Or anything else," Kylie said before swallowing hard.

Maggie watched as Anthony paced slowly back and forth in the other room. It was like the mere mention of David's name set him on edge. It made her wonder if he hadn't just confessed to knowing more about what had happened to his son-in-law than he was letting on.

"I've taken up enough of your time," Maggie

said before taking a sip of water then standing from the table.

"Don't let my dad upset you," Kylie said, looking at her father with dry eyes and a smirk on her lips. "He's from that generation that doesn't have a filter."

"That's called the Greatest Generation," Anthony boasted, his chin held high.

Maggie chuckled and nodded. "Thanks for your time. If I don't see you again, merry Christmas."

They wished Maggie a merry Christmas too as she was escorted to the door. That was when Maggie felt the hairs on her neck stand up and her mouth go dry.

"Didn't I see you before? Were you at the dance at the Elks' Lodge?" Kylie asked and looked at Maggie intensely.

"Yes, I was. Were you there?" Maggie asked, already knowing the answer.

"For a little while. The rumor mill in this town works fast. Maybe it wasn't the right thing to show up. But I'd been behind closed doors for so long that…"

It was the first sign of emotion Maggie had seen from Kylie since she'd walked in the door, and it had nothing to do with David being gone. It had to do with her being free. If what Maggie had seen at the bookstore was any indication of what her life had been like, Maggie wanted to cry with her.

"I was there with the people I worked with," she replied, hoping Kylie might say who she had been there with.

"It was a nice party, but I know people were staring at me. I guess I can't blame them." Kylie sniffed, but no tears fell from her eyes. She'd obviously learned how to control her emotions.

If Maggie could have, she would have given Kylie a hug. Whether or not she'd had anything to do with killing David, it was obvious she was a victim too.

"You should have stayed home with Leo and me," Anthony called from the other room.

Kylie chuckled and shook her head a little. "You never outgrow being Daddy's little girl," she said as if she was really sharing an important secret.

Maggie smiled and shrugged. Before she lost her nerve and spilled the beans about why she was really imposing on the Thornson family, Maggie cleared her throat, thanked Kylie for her time, and left.

As she drove home, she realized she still had David's diary in her car. It didn't really matter now.

She'd dispose of it later. It was only his schedule, and there was nothing of any real importance in it. Everyone knew he had been a lawyer. Everyone knew he had been having an affair. Everyone knew what kind of man he had been.

Chapter 15

It was a surprise to see Gary's squad car pull up in front of Mrs. Peacock's house at the same time Maggie arrived back home.

"Is something wrong with Mrs. Peacock?" Maggie asked as they walked toward each other.

"Aside from being on a fixed income? Not that I'm aware of." Gary smiled.

"So, what are you doing here?"

"She hadn't heard from Mrs. Donovan and wanted me to do a wellness check." Gary shook his head.

"Those two women can't live without each other. Is Mrs. Donovan okay?" Maggie asked, eyebrows raised innocently as she worried the daily diary she possessed would be discovered. She could have sworn it started to feel hot in her hands.

"She's fine. I think Mrs. Peacock's nose was out of joint because Mrs. Donovan hadn't made it to this end of the block to see her light show. NASA can see her lights, but if Mrs. Donovan doesn't see them, they may as well be burned out. That's the Christmas spirit. What have you been up to? Christmas shopping?" Gary asked, leaning back a little as if to see if Maggie had any packages with his name on them.

"Not really. I'm glad you are here. I've got something for you, but it isn't a Christmas present." Maggie took a deep breath and explained every-thing she'd been up to for the past couple of days before handing over the diary.

"Maggie, what you're telling me is that you've committed a handful of offenses, and before I arrest you for one or all of them, you want to turn over evidence you stole," Gary said. He shifted from one leg to the other and put his hands on his waist, just above his utility belt and below the hem of his police-issue winter jacket.

"Yes?" she asked as she handed over the calen-dar. "Your guys left this behind. They didn't see it in the shanty. If anything, I saved your men from looking bad. Now you have it and can do whatever you want with it."

At that moment, a car rolled by slowly. People were looking at the lights down Maggie's street at all hours of the night. When she looked around, she couldn't blame them. The entire block looked as if Las Vegas had added extra lights for Christmas. It really was beautiful. Even the tacky houses with inflatable Peanuts characters or the Grinch looked warm and inviting. But nothing beat Mrs. Peacock's house and her Nativity front and center. Mrs. Donovan's place was lovely in all white lights, but this year was all Mrs. Peacock.

Gary rubbed the back of his neck then pulled his knit cap down a little bit over his ears. "You've put me in a difficult spot, Mags."

"I know," she said.

"I'm going to have to blame it on Larry and Stan and say they shook it loose or something when they decided to move the shack off the ice without permission." He pressed his lips together.

"I don't think there is anything in it that you didn't already know." Maggie smiled as she peeked up from beneath her lashes yet over the tops of her glasses.

Gary chuckled. "You owe me," he said and took

the journal.

"Just name it," Maggie let out a deep breath.

"Oh, this is going to require some thought. You're going to be on the hook for sure. I'll let you know when I come up with something." Gary smirked.

Maggie smiled widely and nodded. She always felt she could be her real awkward self with Gary. They'd known each other so long that she couldn't imagine not seeing him every couple of days.

"Has there been any break in the case?" she asked innocently.

"That's what you really wanted to know, isn't it?" Gary snickered.

He looked up at the sky then over his shoulder at the car that had rolled by and finally turned at the end of the block. It was a Mercedes with tinted windows. Of course, that wasn't odd at all. The people who lived on Mrs. Peacock's block drove very nice cars. In fact, Maggie was fearful the day might come when she'd be asked to take the bus because her junker was too much of an eyesore for the neighbors.

"I'm just curious," Maggie admitted. "No one knows who that man is that Kylie brought to the party. But that's who was at that abandoned building with her. Maybe she was having an affair too."

"Having an affair isn't a crime in the eyes of the law," Gary replied.

"No. But when a spouse turns up dead, it might have something to do with it. I'm just pointing out the obvious."

"Let me ask you something, Mags. You were at the lake when Mr. Thornson and Mr. Campbell got into it. As a casual observer who didn't know either man, what did you think of Mr. Campbell's threats?" Gary took out his pocket notepad and pencil.

Maggie was shocked at the line of questioning. "You don't think he did it, do you? He's a lifelong resident of Fair Haven, and he keeps to himself most of the year. He's a legend with all those ice fishermen, and they respect him. I think you are barking up the wrong tree." Maggie huffed and clasped her hands in front of her.

"We haven't been able to find him. His house is locked up, and no one has seen his truck in a couple of days," Gary said.

"From what I've heard about him, he keeps to himself. No one cares where he is or what he is doing when it isn't ice fishing season or grilling season. The guy is an outdoorsman. Why would someone who barely talks to anyone except a few times a year suddenly lose his cool, knowing he'd be bombarded with attention?" Maggie said.

She didn't have any idea why she felt the need to defend Mr. Campbell except that maybe she felt a certain amount of kinship with him. He was weird and kept to himself. But when he did speak, he had an aura of real confidence and a "no bull" attitude. A man like that just couldn't be a killer.

"Maggie, Jim Campbell has a record. He's run with some bad people and has done some bad things himself. It's my job to investigate all leads, and right now, he *is* one, and he's missing in action," Gary said.

Maggie looked at the decorations on the homes across the street but didn't really see them. She was trying to think of something that would get Gary off Mr. Campbell's scent and start him searching for the guy at the party. Surely, that mystery man was of more interest than the lifelong resident of Fair Haven.

"Wasn't that a long time ago?"

"It doesn't matter, Mags. I've got to do my job. And right now, Mr. Campbell is looking more and more like someone I need to speak with if for no other reason than to cross him off the list. But the longer he's gone, the worse it looks," Gary replied.

Maggie understood and nodded before looking up at her friend, giving him a crooked smile while pushing her glasses up on her nose.

"What's your interest in Mr. Campbell?" Gary asked, catching Maggie off guard.

"I don't know." She shrugged. "He's like a legend around here. Sort of like the Rooster Cogburn of Fair Haven. At least, that's how I see him. Maybe I'm wrong."

"I get it," Gary said. "Let's not make any judgment calls until we find the man. Then we'll see what he has to say. How do you know who Rooster Cogburn is?"

Maggie rolled her eyes then glared at Gary. "I read books, Gary. I read lots of books. Plus, what kind of person doesn't know one of John Wayne's greatest roles? I don't live under a rock."

Gary laughed, making Maggie even more annoyed, so she turned and stomped toward her cottage.

"What?" he called after her. "I was just asking."

"Very funny, Officer Brookes. Very funny," she shouted over her shoulder.

Once Maggie was inside her house, the smile on

her lips slowly slipped away as she thought about what Gary had said about Mr. Campbell. He was too obvious. Didn't Gary see that? Just because a guy got angry didn't mean he was going to shoot someone. Heck, if people were tried and convicted on what they said instead of what they actually did, she'd have been thrown in the hoosegow a dozen times at least for the things she muttered under her breath.

It was still early, and the ice fishermen only had a couple of days of the festival left before the regular ice fishing season took over. The people who had been around Jim Campbell's shanty had been his neighbors on the ice for years. Those were the people Gary should have been talking to. Maybe he already had. But Maggie decided to bundle up and go see what they'd say about the man to someone who wasn't wearing a badge.

Before long, she was back in her car, bundled up under three layers of clothing that included a stocking cap, mittens, and a scarf pulled up almost all the way to her eyes. It wasn't as cold as it had been the other night, but a gentle breeze kept the goose bumps up. Or maybe it was the idea of going to talk to strangers about a man she barely knew. Either way, Maggie shivered.

Chapter 16

Even though the sky was black and the stars were out, it was still early evening, and many of the ice fishermen and -women had come out of their shacks to socialize. Small groups of people gathered, chatting and laughing as they swapped stories of the fish they did or didn't get. People meandered back and forth from the ice to the shore and back again as visitors took in the sight and family members of the diehard ice fishermen brought supplies as well as hugs and kisses. It was easy for Maggie to blend in.

As she walked toward the vacant spot in the ice where David Thornson's shed had been, she was surprised at the nonstop chattering.

"If he didn't have anything to do with it, then

where is he?" one man holding a steaming tin cup said to a small group of others. The man lounged in front of a shanty with a plaque over the door that read A Man's Shack Is His Castle.

"It is strange that he'd be gone. He's missed almost the entire event, and usually, he takes home a trophy. I don't think in the past five years he hasn't placed first or second," said another man with goggle-like glasses.

"Maybe he's sick. Has anyone tried his house?" came a female voice from deep inside a shapeless parka and snow pants.

"Jim Campbell doesn't get sick. He gets even," said the last man in the group, who was holding a fishing rod.

"I'm telling you what happened," Mr. Tin Cup said before clearing his throat. "That smart-alecky lawyer needled him after the law left. Old Jim went back to his shack, got his rifle, and popped him. Then reality set in and he left town. End of story."

"Wouldn't there have been some evidence left behind?" the woman asked.

"What more evidence than him leaving town do you need?" Tin Cup replied.

"I don't know. I've been on the ice for over six years, and Jim has been nothing but quiet and polite. I find it hard to believe a guy like him would do that," the woman continued.

"Are you kidding? That's what they said about Ted Bundy. The guy was too handsome and charming to be a killer. Yet he did it." Tin Cup lifted his chin after he spoke.

Again with Ted Bundy, Maggie thought. She wondered what the fascination with Ted Bundy was. It seemed that whenever there was an issue, the armchair detectives always compared their suspect to Ted Bundy. Not only had the guy been dead for years, but there had been worse men since to make comparisons to. Maggie knew this because she'd read her fair share of crime stories from the bookstore. Not to mention she was pretty sure Mr. Campbell had not tried to charm David Thornson. That stuff only worked when the victims were female. At least, that was Maggie's theory, and she would readily admit to being always suspicious of everyone.

"Ted Bundy? Jim is nothing like Ted Bundy. What is wrong with you?" the woman scoffed.

"Yeah. What are you talking about?" Goggle Glasses said. "Look, we only know what we know. That lawyer took Jim's spot, and I can't help but think it was on purpose. Jim had a lawsuit going, and the rumor is that Thornson was the opposing party's lawyer."

Maggie gasped behind her scarf as she busied herself with a lace on her thick snow boots. This was a new development. Gary had to know it. Yet he hadn't breathed a word to her. Oh, she was going to have some words with him the next time she saw him. Keeping secrets from his oldest friend? That was not cool.

"He was a divorce lawyer," the woman replied. "Jim's been divorced for years. What could that be about?"

"Jim has more than one ex-wife too. You just never know with these women," Goggle Glasses stated.

"What was the lawsuit about?" Tin Cup asked before taking a sip from his tin cup.

"I can't say for sure, but I heard it was over some land that Jim owned and hadn't disclosed during the brief marriage to the last wife. Now she was claiming half of it was hers and he'd have to buy her out or something like that. I can't say for sure," Goggles replied and shrugged.

"How do you know this?" the woman asked.

"Hey, I hear things," Goggles said and chuckled.

"You've been awfully quiet, Steve. What do you think happened?" Tin Cup asked the last man in the group, who had almost disappeared into the scenery because he was so quiet.

Maggie casually looked at the man as if she was looking past him for someone else. He was a scruffy guy with the start of a wild beard and thick eyebrows.

"I think that lawyer got what was coming to him, and I think it is exactly the way you said," Steve replied. His voice was deep and thoughtful.

Maggie thought he was the strong, silent type who could spot a flim-flam artist from a mile away because he'd either been one himself or had led the kind of life that exposed him to a lot.

"Jim did tell me about his ex-wife. He also said he would have been happy to settle it with her, but she went and got a lawyer involved. Apparently, that half-pint attorney liked to harass the opposition. It isn't the first time since he arrived in town that he has done stuff just to keep the other attorneys off balance. I heard he started dating one of his clients after he got her off stalking charges. Just to stick it to the opposing side."

"Thornson was married," the woman said. "That sounds like a lot of horse hockey to me."

Steve shrugged. Maggie watched them from beneath the fuzzy brim of her cap. Careful not to look as if she was still eavesdropping she stretched her neck to the right and left, stood on her tiptoes, and pretended to look at a watch that wasn't on her wrist.

"Right, because married men never cheat on their wives," Steve replied without a shred of emotion in his voice.

"I've seen Thornson's wife," Tin Cup said and let out a whistle. "From what I've heard, she is really nice too. Too good for the likes of him is what people are saying."

"As much as I like Jim, I'm afraid that he let his temper get the best of him. We don't know what other things he might have been dealing with. His ex-wife might have just been the latest drama. Add any sort of aggravation plus her attorney taking his real estate here on the ice that he'd had for at least a decade, and you just might have the perfect storm," Steve said. "And we all know he's crossed the law before. Push any man far enough and he'll break."

When the conversation turned to who was winning in the ice fishing competition, Maggie shuffled across the ice to listen in on a few more conversations. The topics ranged from Christmas dinners to what the weather was predicting in snow to local politics. But it seemed that eventually, the conversation turned to poor Jim Campbell, whose absence equaled his guilt.

"I've known Jim and been with him through rough times. He's a tough old bird, but his rowdy days are long over. He gave up that lifestyle when he sold his Harley," said another bearded man in a snowsuit that was peeled off his arms, hanging from his waist but still covering his legs. He towered over everyone else and had a barrel chest covered in flannel.

If Maggie had had to guess, the man tipped the scales at about three hundred fifty pounds, and it wasn't just fat.

"Do you ever give up that lifestyle?" The woman who asked that question had a round, red nose and cheeks. Her hair was kinky like a poodle's and hung down around her face, pushed close by the orange stocking cap she wore. She had a pole in one hand and a cooler in the other.

"Not usually," the big man replied. "If he did do anything, then Jim was pushed to it. Of that I have no doubt."

"Unfortunately, the law doesn't see things that way," the red-nosed woman replied.

"No. If Ol' Boy did have something to do with this, they are going to see his record, and it will be good night, Irene. He had a past that wasn't the cleanest," Mr. Snowsuit said.

"I've heard that. Heck, I've heard him admit to it. That still doesn't mean he did it. It just means he's the kind of guy who *would* do it," the red-nosed woman added.

They continued their conversation and, like the others, said a whole lot of nothing that the police or anyone else could hang their hat on.

As Maggie walked around and listened, she quickly realized the discussions about Mr. Campbell and David Thornson didn't vary much in substance. Jim Campbell certainly could have committed murder. If he didn't have a hand in what had happened to David, where the heck was he?

One common thread wove through all of it: everyone seemed to agree that it couldn't have happened to a better guy. No tears were shed for David Thornson. It was as if it had all been analyzed, and the jury was hung. No one seemed to have any more information about the murder than what Maggie had already known.

Sure, she got a few new facts, like Thornson provoking his opposition and that everyone knew about his affair with Gretchen. But what Maggie found interesting was that everyone seemed to think that Mr. Campbell was the only one capable of such a crime. No one looked to Kylie or the man she had flaunted at the Jubilee Dance.

Maybe "flaunted" isn't the right word. But she certainly didn't practice discretion, Maggie thought. She really liked Kylie, but maybe that was what a murderess wanted. The innocent babe-in-the-woods routine was as old as the hills and still worked.

Chapter 17

With the wind having died down to nothing but an occasional draft and the protection of several layers of clothes, Maggie decided as she walked to her car that she wanted to look again at that building she'd seen Kylie in. The snow along the sidewalk had a dry path that led the way. As she stood in front of the majestic old structure, she tried to remember what it had looked like in the daytime. It was a piece of history, with beautiful architecture and stories that unfolded in every room. It wasn't the creepy, haunted-looking place it was now, half engulfed in pitch-black shadows with nothing but the scurrying of mice and the flutter of pigeons to wake the spirits that had lain dormant for so long.

"It's just an empty building," Maggie said to herself as she looked down at her feet and strolled down the gangway. That was when she saw something that didn't seem right. A single set of footprints in the snow that led to the back of the house was a perfect match to the boots she was wearing at the moment. It was the only trace of her left behind from when she had followed Kylie's mystery man into the building.

But now there was a much larger set of footprints next to hers. Was it from the man in the green-and-yellow Green Bay Packers cap? Maggie thought for a moment.

"No. Those would have been coming from the other direction," Maggie muttered. These size twelves followed alongside her tracks. They also looked fresher, as if maybe they had just been made a short while ago.

She looked up at the house. What was she searching for? Maybe a pair of beady red eyes peeking back at her? Was she expecting to hear a wail or the howl of a pitiful lost soul trapped among the rafters for all eternity?

Her heart jumped as she saw the eerie white glow shining through the crooked slats of the boarded-up windows.

Maggie swallowed hard. She looked across the street and saw a bundled-up couple slowly strolling down the sidewalk. There was no full moon looming overhead, no claps of thunder after a shock of lightning. Off in the distance, she heard only a couple car horns. No howling wolves or desperate screams. It was a regular December night in Fair Haven, with a smell of snow in the air and the twinkling of Christmas lights around every corner.

"There isn't anything to be scared of. Someone is in that building, that's all," Maggie said. "It's probably the mystery man Kylie had been hiding in plain sight."

Steeling her nerves, Maggie squared her shoulders and went around the back of the building, where she'd gone before. This time, she stayed in the shadows and stopped every couple of steps and listened for anyone else crunching on the snow. As she made her way up the steps to the back door, she leaned toward it, hoping to hear something not terrifying on the other side.

With only a slight touch against the thick wood, there was movement. She nearly let out a scream of her own when the door slowly slid open.

Whoever was inside hadn't closed the door all

the way. Perhaps they were waiting for someone else to join them. Could this be the place where Kylie and her mystery man met for romantic evenings alone? Did they come here for quick trysts and then head off to their respective homes? Weren't they cold? Maybe this was their plan until the heat of David's murder died down or an innocent man like Jim Campbell was arrested for the act.

"You don't know he's innocent, Maggie. You just think he looks like the hero of some western. Get your head together," she muttered as she peeked into the darkness.

Inhaling deeply and holding her breath, Maggie slowly pushed the door open a little farther, wincing at the soft squeak of the old hinges that was trying to give her away. As soon as she was inside, she shivered. It wasn't surprising to detect the smell of mold and mothballs. But Maggie also detected smoke. Cigarette smoke. And she could hear the creak of boards in a room just ahead.

As her eyes adjusted to the darkness, some of the features of the house became clearer. She was in what people called a mudroom. Just beyond it was probably a kitchen based on the cabinets she saw in a faint ray of light from the street. Beyond that was pitch darkness.

Maggie was scared. She had read her fair share of horror stories, and the image of a white, ghoulish face peering at her from the shadows was dancing relentlessly around the corners of her thoughts. She tried to remain calm and remember that it was Christmastime, the most wonderful time of the year, as the song proclaimed. She tried to recite the words to that old song to distract herself as she listened. There wasn't anything to be scared of.

Just take a couple steps forward down the hallway and see what you can, her conscience urged. The man pacing across the same slats of hardwood told her with each groan that he was preoccupied.

The soles of her thick snow boots cushioned each step as she slowly walked heel to toe down the hallway. She could hear the soft mumblings of a male voice. As she strained to make out what he was saying, Maggie thought maybe she'd stumbled across a homeless person who was arguing with the voices in his head.

With her hands stretched out to keep her balance as she walked down the short hallway to the kitchen, Maggie saw the gray light in the room ahead brighten. Was he coming in her direction? She froze.

Up ahead, at the end of the dark hallway, she saw the silhouette of a man in a long coat, no hat, and hard shoes not meant for walking in the snow. He didn't look down the hallway. A battery-operated lantern dangled from his hand. That was obviously the light she'd seen from the street.

"You don't know what you've done," he muttered. "We can make it work, but I need your help. I can't do this alone. You've got to see that."

The conversation was low, one-sided, and angry. It was as if he was pacing back and forth while talking on the phone. But there was no phone in this place.

Maggie slowed her breathing and listened. All thoughts of ghosts and evil red eyes peering at her had disappeared. This man was distraught and might need help. After another slow step toward the end of the hallway, her arms still outstretched, Maggie turned her head to listen better.

"It was all planned. It turned out perfectly. Don't you see? Don't you understand what this means?" he continued his conversation with himself.

Maggie pressed herself against the wall, her palms flat against the dusty, cobwebbed wall, and shuffled silently a few more steps to try to get a glimpse of the man who was talking.

When she peeked, she saw he was wearing an expensive long wool coat the color of sand. His hair was dark and slicked back. His shoes were dressy and clomped on the floor with each slow, deliberate step. He had a barrel chest, and Maggie was positive he wasn't Kylie's mystery man. They were completely different body types, and this guy in the expensive wool coat looked like he could eat the mystery man for breakfast.

"It's such a small request. I love you. I love you. Don't you know that? Can't you see it?" he continued before checking his watch. "You're late again. But I'll wait. You know I'll wait. I always do, and you always let me down. After everything I've done for you. You still let me down like you enjoy torturing me."

It wasn't hard in the silence of the house to detect the shift in the man's tone. He kept his back to her, but Maggie could hear the anger welling inside him. Whoever he was having this imaginary conversation with was starting to get on his nerves. But why in the world would he come to this place to have this one-sided conversation?

Suddenly, he turned and started to walk toward the hallway Maggie was hiding in.

She pressed her body against the wall and sucked in her gut as if she could conceal herself in the dirty patterned and peeling wallpaper. For a split second, she squeezed her eyes shut, but the fear of having him suddenly in front of her, his breath on her face and his massive form boxing her in, was too much. She popped her eyes open, half expecting to see him standing there, staring at her like a bull ready to charge. But he wasn't there.

"I think you are so beautiful. Just so beautiful. I know what you've been through. I understand, and you can trust me. I've been…"

Just then, Maggie shifted, causing the floor-board to groan. She may as well have just shouted *Yoo-hoo! Over here!* All she could hear was her heart pounding in her chest. It was as if she was suddenly standing in front of a blast furnace. Her heart raced like an excited guinea pig in an exercise wheel, and sweat instantly formed along the middle of her back.

"Kylie?" the man called.

For a split second, Maggie felt her feet grow roots into the dirty, scuffed floor. She was paralyzed with fear. This huge man who mumbled to himself was going to march right over here, shine that light in her face, and then God knew what when he realized she wasn't Kylie. Why did he think she *was* Kylie?

Move, Mags! Move! Run! her mind screamed.

It was like watching a film in slow motion. Maggie gasped, turned toward the mudroom, and started to run. Her boots galumphed across the floor while her arms waved madly as if she were shooing bees. Her eyes were wide and wild, and her mouth was open as she made it to the back door. With all her might, she pushed it open, jumped over the steps, then felt the sharp pain of landing on the hard surface shoot up her ankles and shins. Without waiting for the throb to subside, she staggered to the hole in the fence. Once in the alley, she gulped the cold, crisp air and bent over with her hands on her knees.

But before she could catch her breath, the man appeared in the doorway. "Kylie," he hissed as if he didn't want to shout out loud and alert anyone he was there.

Maggie pulled herself together and took off running toward the street and where she'd parked her car. That man was in hard-soled shoes. It would be impossible for him to maneuver in the snow to follow her.

When she finally made it to her car, she climbed in, locked the doors, started the engine, and cranked the heat. Even though she was sweating from her close call, she felt a chill sweeping over her shoulders. As she looked out the back window and both side windows in all directions, Maggie's body shook with adrenaline and cold. No one appeared to be following her.

The puffs of steam coming from her mouth as she caught her breath curled up around her face and fogged the window slightly.

"Who was that guy?" she muttered, the sound of her own voice shocking her a little. It was so much more solid than the voice in her head. Even when her thoughts were telling her to run, there was a transparency to them, as if they could be blown away with a single breath. When she spoke out loud, she knew she was there, alone, alive, in her car and safe.

"And why did he think I was Kylie? I can't imagine there are many women named Kylie in this town. And even if there were a dozen of them, why would they be meeting another man in the same dilapidated building?"

She turned on her headlights, only to see the hulking man who had been in the house standing right there in her high beams.

Chapter 18

Maggie's eyes bulged. "Aaahhh!" she screamed. She threw the car into reverse and pulled out of the parking spot.

The man just stood there, his chest heaving as he glared at her.

She'd never seen him before in her life. Without thinking, she put the car in drive and hit the gas, speeding out of there and away from the lake, the old brownstone, and the man who had somehow been able to keep up with her.

"Oh my gosh!" she panted. "What the heck? How did he follow me? He's like three hundred pounds! Am I not as agile as I think I am? What the heck? Oh, Mags, this is not good! Not good at all!"

she shouted in her car. Looking in the rearview mirror, she saw a couple sets of headlights behind her. Any one of them could be that man. If he could practically beam himself to that parking lot, it would be stupid to think he wasn't already in his car and in pursuit.

"What do I do? What do I do?" she muttered before looking at her gas gauge and taking a deep breath. She had more than half a tank. She could drive to the next county if she wanted to throw him off her scent—if he was behind her.

But as if on cue, snow flurries started to fall. There was no way she was going to drive around if the weather was about to change. She could go to the police department. That was it. She'd go there and tell them what happened.

"Sure, Maggie. Go tell them you were trespassing on private property in the old, dangerous brownstone, spying on a guy who you knew was in there because you are sticking your nose into a murder investigation that doesn't concern you in the slightest. All because you have some kind of teenage crush on Jim Campbell, the guy they suspect is a killer, and you can't believe he could be guilty. Sure, that sounds logical. Gary won't slap you with half a dozen misdemeanor charges and probably not talk to you for months if not longer."

She huffed as she looked in her side mirror. So far, none of the cars behind her were tailgating or acting threatening.

Maybe he wasn't behind her after all. Still, she didn't want to go to her home and lead the guy to her front door. Instead, she went to the bookstore. From the street, she could see the warm glow of the fireplace in the apartment above the shop. Joshua was home. He'd help her. Or at least he'd not throw her in jail for obstructing justice or interfering in a murder investigation.

But after she spilled the beans to him, she wasn't sure going to the police wouldn't have been the better idea.

"You did what?" Joshua barked as his eyebrows shot up to his hairline.

"Hey, he was in that building first. Maybe you should talk to him about trespassing." Maggie pinched her eyebrows together as she took a seat.

He'd made some subtle changes to the apartment since the last time she'd been upstairs. A couple new photographs on the wall had replaced some paintings Maggie had never been all that impressed with. There was a new leather La-Z-Boy recliner and a new stereo in the corner that looked a little out of place among all the antiquities and vintage items. Maggie wanted to ask Joshua what he thought he was doing making changes to his father's apartment but thought better of it. It wasn't her home, and it wasn't Mr. Whitfield's home anymore either. It was Joshua's, and he could do what he wanted.

"Maybe he owns the building. Did you ever think of that, Sherlock?" Joshua said as he came from the kitchen with a teapot and poured hot water into a cup of instant hot chocolate.

"Then why were Kylie Thornson and her mystery man in there the other day?" Maggie snapped back before realizing what she was saying.

"How do you know Kylie Thornson was there with a mystery man?" Joshua asked, his eyebrows making a "V" shape.

"Because…I…followed him?" Maggie said and swallowed.

Just as she was about to reach for a handful of mini marshmallows to drop into her hot chocolate, Joshua snatched the bag away. "Why would you do that? Maggie, that is crazy! Not only could you have followed a dangerous person, but you could have gotten hurt in that building. Forget that your mystery man might have been a sadistic murderer. There could have been tweakers or hobos or escaped convicts hiding out in there. You could have fallen through the floor or had a loose light fixture fall on your head. I wouldn't know what had happened to you! How would I have found you?"

"He's not really *my* mystery man. He's Kylie Thornson's mystery man," Maggie said. She raised her thumb to her lips and chewed her nail for a second.

"I'm not joking, Maggie. What would I have done if something happened to you?" Joshua set the bag of marshmallows back down on the coffee table in front of the couch where they were sitting.

"Come on. Nothing happened. Besides, it wouldn't be that hard to replace me. There are plenty of women who want to work at the bookstore." Maggie wanted to rattle off the names of ladies in town who eyeballed the single, attractive, and successful bachelor running the Bookish Café. For starters, Joyce from the bank would have been happy to cut her pay in half if it meant getting a chance at an engagement ring from Joshua. Even if she had to hogtie him and torture him, Joyce wouldn't go down without a fight.

"How can you even say that?" Joshua said as if

Maggie had just slapped him across the face with a cold, scaly fish.

"I just meant that what I do is hardly brain surgery. Anyone could…"

"No, Maggie. Not anyone. In fact, no one else could do what you do. You make that whole bookstore come alive. You treat each book with respect so everyone who comes in knows they are coming into a special place. I don't know anyone else who could do that. And if you were gone…if I didn't know where you were, I…" Joshua looked at her with hard eyes and not even a hint of a smirk on his face. When he sat down next to her, he let out a sigh.

Maggie swallowed hard. Her chest felt like there was a ball of tangled Christmas lights in there. This was a reaction she hadn't been prepared for. It was as if she was seeing a different person in front of her. She looked down at her hands before reaching for the cup of hot chocolate.

There had been a handful of times when she'd sat on this same couch with Alexander Whitfield, talking and sharing a pot of soup or even just some tea or hot chocolate on a cold night like this. But sitting here with Joshua did not feel the same. In fact, it felt hard, jagged, like she was trying to squeeze through automatic doors that were determined to close whether there was a person stuck in the middle or not. There was no way she was going to get through without getting a little dirty and jostled around. Had she known he'd get so upset, she wouldn't have said anything. Heck, she wouldn't have gone snooping at all.

"I'm sorry," Maggie said. The words came out of her mouth before they even registered in her head.

"No. I shouldn't have yelled at you like that," Joshua said.

"No. You are right. I wasn't thinking, and that was careless of me to go snooping around in the dark without letting anyone know where I was." Maggie nodded.

"I don't know why you'd think people don't worry about you. Jeez, I worry about you all the time," Joshua admitted with a smirk on his lips.

"You do? What for?" Maggie asked, wrinkling her nose and pushing her glasses up.

"I don't know. I worry that you aren't having fun at work like you did when my father was alive. That you don't realize how much I appreciate what you do or that I don't realize how smart you are," he said before looking down at his own mug of hot chocolate, which had cooled on the table.

"I'm having fun at work," Maggie assured Joshua and put one hand on his forearm. "I'm still shocked at the number of people who buy those paperbacks you stock up on. *The Delta Variant* or *Amber's Reason*. They are so bad." Maggie chuckled nervously before Joshua put his hand on hers. Then she froze.

"I know they are a lot simpler than most of the books *you've* read. But you are special that way, Maggie. That's what makes you stand out from everyone else." Joshua squeezed her hand.

Maggie quickly pulled her hand away and wrapped it around her mug before she raised it to her lips and took a sip. The cocoa tasted delicious, but she would have preferred a glass of ice-cold water. That feeling of being in front of a blast furnace overcame her again, but it wasn't caused by fear. Or maybe it was. Maybe Maggie was afraid of how she was feeling now for Joshua. He wasn't just some guy. He was her boss. He was the son of Mr. Whitfield, her dearest friend. What would people think?

"I better get going," Maggie said with her eyes down and her chin tucked in.

"Oh, well, why don't you let me drive you home," Joshua said.

"No, I think enough time has gone by. There p- probably isn't even anyone following me," she stuttered.

"Just to be on the safe side," Joshua insisted with a smile as if that was the end of the discussion.

"No. I can handle myself," she insisted.

"I know you can, Maggie. But you made some bad decisions tonight. Make a good one and let me take you home." Joshua tittered as he stood from the couch, smoothed out his pants, and stepped around the coffee table. He headed toward his coat, which was hanging next to the door.

"I think a good idea is to drive myself home," she replied with a huff.

"Maggie, you are so stubborn! Just let me take you home!"

"I don't need you to take me home! Jeez, I'm not a child!"

"I didn't say you were! I just thought you were scared when you showed up here, and so I was trying to make you feel safe. Forgive the heck out of me!" Joshua shook his head as he put one hand against the wall and the other on his hip.

Maggie fussed with her coat. The sleeves had

gotten pulled through the wrong way. But it wasn't just her coat that had her flustered. It was this whole conversation. Of course she wanted Joshua to take her home. But then what? He'd walk her to her door—or worse, come inside. The whole idea made her tremble. She wasn't afraid of the man outside anymore. In fact, she would have welcomed a run-in with the guy instead of this tidal wave of anxiety that had washed over her.

"Let me help you with that," Joshua said as he reached for Maggie's coat.

She snatched it away from him like a child having a tantrum. "I've got it," she muttered.

"You do not!" Joshua chuckled and snatched the coat out of her hands completely.

Maggie stood there with her arms at her sides, her delicate hands clenched into fists. She squinted at Joshua as he pulled the sleeves out the correct way. Part of her wanted nothing more than to slap that smirk off his face. The other half wanted to kiss it away. Those feelings battled it out inside while she stood stone still, glaring over the top of her glasses at Joshua, who was smiling.

Then he did the worst thing. He held her jacket open for her.

Her heart raced, and she didn't know if it was

from excitement or anger. If her ego had not been participating, Maggie would have taken a step back, taken a deep breath, and collected herself. But her ego had grown into a six-foot-seven Amazon who was ready to fight anyone over anything. She stretched out her hand while pursing her lips and demanded her coat without saying a word.

"I'll help you with your coat, Maggie," Joshua said, still smirking and looking so adorable and handsome that Maggie wanted to scream.

Who did he think he was? She let out a sigh, her shoulders dropped, and she was sure she saw her brain when she rolled her eyes so hard. She turned around and let Joshua slip her coat up her arms and over her shoulders. Before she could do anything, he spun her around, tugged the coat tight around her, put her scarf gently around her neck, and, finally, pulled her hood up.

"I know how to dress myself," Maggie mumbled. The venom had been forced out of her voice by the pounding of her heart pushing the adrenaline through her veins. She was sure Joshua could hear her heart beating or feel it through the fabric of her coat.

"Would you call me when you get home and let me know you made it?" Joshua asked softly.

Maggie nodded, pulled her mittens from her pockets, grabbed the doorknob, and quickly left. Had she looked behind her once on her way to her car, she would have seen Joshua watching from the bookstore door.

All the way home, Maggie huffed and pouted over Joshua's behavior. It wasn't that she had completely forgotten about the stranger in the long tan coat who had stood in front of her car, his barrel chest heaving like an animal's. She just didn't want to think about it. Not while it was still dark outside.

Chapter 19

The next morning, Maggie arrived at the bookstore to find a pleasant surprise taped to the door. *The Bookish Café will be closed for our 1st Christmas Party*. The same note was taped to the café entrance. She let herself into the bookstore and locked the door behind her before she heard the laughter and chatter from the café.

"Maggie! Isn't this great?" Babs had one of the specialty drinks in front of her. Maggie couldn't tell what it was, but it was piled high with whipped cream, chocolate and caramel drizzles, and a cherry on top.

"Did you know about this?" Maggie asked. She stuffed her mittens into her pockets, unwound her scarf, and pulled off her jacket.

"Nope. Neither did Roy. He's got the baby, and they are running errands all day. Don't get me wrong. I love my men, but Mama could use a break from both of them. Come! Sit! Casper and I are enjoying a hazelnut coffee-caramel-chocolate delight with extra whipped cream."

"Where is Casper?" Maggie asked. She walked over and took a seat at the quaint table for two, where Babs had pulled a chair out for her.

"He's getting more cherries," Babs giggled.

Christmas songs played throughout both shops. When Casper appeared with a jar of maraschino cherries and a Santa hat, even Maggie had to smile. He looked adorable as he spoke softly, telling the ladies that he'd bought a necklace-and-earring set for his girlfriend and a book and a couple of stuffed animals and a whole list of little things that girls loved.

"Now, I'm not sure what your plans are for Christmas, Mags," Babs said. "I know your sister isn't coming in, and, well, with Mr. Whitfield celebrating Jesus's birthday *with* Jesus, Roy and I wanted to invite you to our house for Christmas. We've got a revolving door at this time of the year. Believe me, there will be more than enough food, and even if you just wanted to stop by to fix yourself a plate to take home, we'd love it!"

"That's really thoughtful of you, Babs." Maggie couldn't help but smile. "I'd love to stop by."

"Great!" Babs clapped. "That means everyone from here is coming. I've got oodles of family that come from four different states, and so does Roy. Of course, everyone wants to see the baby." Babs rolled her eyes. "But can you blame them? He's such a little sweet potato."

Maggie laughed as she listened to Babs talk while she fixed her a hazelnut-caramel-chocolate delight with extra whipped cream. It was as delicious as it looked. Thankfully, as Maggie sat at the small table, her coworkers did most of the talking and didn't ask too many questions. She didn't feel like talking, but she did enjoy listening. It was one of the things she truly missed with Mr. Whitfield being gone. He would give his opinions on certain books, dissecting characters and settings and foreshadowing or symbolism, and Maggie would hang on every word.

It suddenly struck her that the murder in town had been on her mind so much that she had forgotten this would be her first Christmas without Mr. Whitfield. A lump formed in her throat. The last thing she wanted to do was start crying in front of everyone.

But as if he was reading her mind, Joshua suddenly appeared, also wearing a Santa hat like Casper. "Ho ho ho!" he shouted as he walked into the café with a small red bag in his right hand.

Maggie frowned at him. Why he didn't tell her last night that she wasn't going to have to work she didn't know. He was looking at her like the cat that had swallowed the canary. The annoyance Joshua made her feel chased away her urge to get teary, and Maggie was grateful.

"So, what are we doing, Josh?" Babs asked.

"Yeah. Are we spending the day laughing at the shoppers who yank on the doors but can't get in?" Casper asked.

"Not quite. I wasn't sure if we'd be able to have a Christmas party, but after doing the books and setting a few things aside since I arrived, we not only have enough to have a Christmas party but"— he shook the red bag—"a little something extra from Santa this year."

Mr. Whitfield had always managed to give Maggie a little gift during Christmas. Even though she knew the bookstore wasn't making any kind of real profit, Alexander Whitfield was like Santa

Claus. She'd get a couple extra bucks and usually an obscure title from some author she'd never heard of. The book was usually old, frayed around the edges, with the name of some stranger written in pencil on the inside cover.

"I found this at the thrift store on Rice Street." Mr. Whitfield would chuckle and then give her a blurb that would entice her to read the book as soon as she got home, which she usually did. A lively discussion would take place the day after the holiday. It was their tradition.

"And that's not all," Joshua said. "I've invited a couple of people from town to come for a private showing of our little shop and our amazing display window, which has captured the attention of some prominent locals." Joshua smiled when he looked at Maggie.

"We have prominent locals?" Casper joked.

"We have a couple." Joshua laughed. "And we have a couple of bookworms who are interested in some of the first editions we've got. They'll be coming around noon, and the others will…"

Just then, there was a knock on the door. The Marys had cupped their hands over the glass and were peering in. They waved wildly with flyers in their hands and giggled loudly like they always did.

"The others will be coming throughout the morning. They have to have a ticket like these lovely ladies do," Joshua said. He waved back and opened the door for them.

"This is such a wonderful idea!" Mary Jean squealed as she gave her flyer to Joshua. "We absolutely love your bookstore. It has some of the most fascinating things in it."

"You've got a beautiful book on the early sketches of Picasso that I was debating if I should buy. Then I got your flyer. I think it was a message from heaven." Mary Anne chuckled.

"Welcome, ladies. You know where everything is. And we've got complimentary coffee for you if you like too." Joshua smiled and stretched his arm in the direction of the bookstore.

The women gushed as they shuffled to the bookstore, happy to have the place to themselves for a while.

As the Marys busied themselves in the bookstore, Joshua had one more surprise for his employees. "I managed to get us a table at Paulie's. Dinner is on me. If you don't mind eating at two in the afternoon in the bar area, because they were booked with Christmas parties all day and night." Joshua laughed.

Paulie's was a fancy restaurant that had linen tablecloths and napkins, a crystal chandelier in the lobby over a marble floor, and a menu that didn't list prices.

Maggie looked down at her clothes and was very self-conscious about her outfit for such a fancy place. She didn't have the hourglass figure that Babs did that enabled her to go anywhere and look glamorous.

"Are we dressed okay for that place?" Casper asked as he looked down at his own blue jeans and frayed red sweater.

"Are you kidding?" Joshua smirked. "We not only have the most beautiful window on the main drag, but I've got the best-looking staff in Fair Haven."

Maggie couldn't help but notice how he looked at her when he said that. Her cheeks flushed, and she did what she always did: wrinkled her nose and squinted. Then she got up and went into the bookstore to help the Marys.

Even though they didn't have regular customers coming into the store, it was a steady stream, every hour, of special customers holding their special flyers coming in to find that special gift for a loved one.

Then Maggie saw a face she wasn't expecting. Tapping on the glass, looking in with twinkling crystal-blue eyes, was Mr. Campbell.

She hurried to the door, snapped the lock, and pulled the door open, trying not to stare at him as if she was some kid in awe of her favorite celebrity. She didn't even know the man. She'd only seen him around town a handful of times, and the words he had said to her that day in the coffee shop were the extent of her conversations with him.

"Morning," he said as he stepped into the shop, looking down at least eight inches to Maggie's upturned face.

"Good morning and merry Christmas," Maggie said before swallowing hard.

"Mr. Campbell," Joshua called before appearing from behind one of the bookcases. "Congratulations are in order."

Maggie didn't hide her confusion. She stepped back to allow Joshua to shake Jim's hand like they were old friends.

"Well, thank you, son. Yup, she had a baby boy. Nine pounds eleven ounces. My daughter is only five foot four. How she managed a butterball like that I don't know. But everyone is doing just fine. I'll be heading back up that way once the weather says I can." Mr. Campbell beamed.

He had been out of town to be with his daughter, who had had a baby.

"And what did they name him?" Joshua asked.

Mr. Campbell seemed to stand even taller as he cleared his throat and grinned. "James. James Bradford. Can you believe it?"

Maggie watched the emotion surface in the man's eyes.

"That's just great, Jim. Thanks to Maggie here, we've got some great books for the little ones. Go nuts," Joshua said, motioning toward the kids' section.

"I'll do just that. Thank you, sir," Jim replied and went over to the kids' section. A man like him didn't worry what people thought. But as he wiped a tear of joy off his cheek, Maggie smiled.

"How do you know him?" Maggie quietly asked Joshua after tugging on his sleeve and stepping out of Mr. Campbell's view.

"I meet people, Maggie. And I tell them about the bookstore and café. And I find out that almost everyone in this town likes to read, and if they don't, they know someone who does." He winked.

"I didn't need the sarcastic tone," Maggie huffed.

"I'm not being sarcastic." Joshua chuckled.

"Of course you are. That's what you do. You get sarcastic and then act like you didn't do anything." Maggie huffed before stepping closer to Joshua to whisper, "Gary was looking for him. You know, because of that whole ice fishing murder thingie. He was considered a suspect. Does he know he's back in town?"

"I don't know. Why don't you go tell Jim yourself that he should go let Gary know he's back in town?" Joshua whispered back.

"Are you daft? I wouldn't look at him cross-eyed," Maggie replied, carefully looking over her shoulder in Mr. Campbell's direction.

"Why? He's a nice man," Joshua said.

"I saw him at the lake the night David Thornson was murdered," Maggie said. "He didn't come across as the kind of man who took any fluff from anyone. Plus you know the rumors. He was in a biker gang. Did some time in jail. I don't know. He scares me a little. Even if he does look like an old cowboy."

"Yeah, the rumor mill in Fair Haven gets a lot of facts wrong," Joshua said. He touched Maggie's arm tenderly and returned to the café to chat with the Marys, who had bought a dozen books between them and were enjoying their free coffee.

Maggie lifted her chin and stepped to the counter, where Poe was enjoying a warm square of sunshine. She scratched the cat's head, watching his eyes close and hearing his purring like a little motor in his chest.

Mr. Campbell finally reappeared with a handful of books about diggers, firemen, and cowboys. The pictures were bright and the words were simple, making Maggie smile.

"You boys ought to have fun reading these together," she said.

"You know it," Mr. Campbell replied. "Did you do that window?"

"Yes. Part of my job is to decorate the windows for the holidays or special occasions." Maggie shrugged.

"I think that's the prettiest display out of all of them. I saw it when I was on my way to the lake the other night," he said.

For a second Maggie froze, wondering if he'd heard what she'd said about letting Gary know he was back or that David Thornson had been killed.

"Did you get in any ice fishing?" she asked innocently.

"Naw. Too busy becoming a grandpa. Ice fishing is great, but I think being called Grandpa is better." He smiled proudly.

"Now you'll have someone to take with you," Maggie said as she bagged up his purchases and handed them over.

"You know it. Merry Christmas." He nodded and went into the café for his free coffee.

Maggie watched him leave and felt a wave of relief, not just because he was the kind of man that kept a person on their toes but because he had an alibi. His daughter having a baby was easy enough to confirm. No one would lie about such a thing, would they? Well, someone might, but not Mr. Campbell.

As the time slipped by, work felt more like a party than anything. Maggie happily chatted with some of the special customers who had the special flyer to shop. The people who were interested in the first editions they had on display behind glass were a pleasant couple in their late sixties taking a vacation from Boston. They didn't buy the book Joshua had discussed with them over the phone, making

Maggie feel as if they were rejecting the bookstore somehow.

"Don't let it get to you," Joshua whispered just after they left for the café. "They didn't want to pay what I was asking. I'll bet in a couple weeks, they'll be back and accept my offer."

"Really?" Maggie was surprised at Joshua's reply.

"You aren't the only one who knows how to research something." He winked, making Maggie pinch her lips together and shake her head.

Finally, at one o'clock, a couple people from the *Fair Haven Bugle* came with their camera and a pad a of paper to get some information about the young woman who had decorated the window of the Bookish Café.

Although Maggie didn't like being questioned and gave one-word answers for almost everything, she did manage to elaborate on one thing.

"I just thought that in between all the shopping, people should take a minute to remember why they are buying a gift for someone they love." She shrugged, pushed up her glasses, and squinted awkwardly at the reporter.

They thanked her for her time, thanked Joshua, and enjoyed a free cup of coffee from the café.

Maggie was glad it was over. She had started to sweat and was sure that her deodorant was going to give out at any minute.

After a few niceties, Joshua ushered everyone outside, locked up the shops, and handed out directions to Paulie's Restaurant.

Chapter 20

After a couple wrong turns and a few cuss words, Maggie made it to Paulie's Restaurant and saw everyone waiting outside for her. Casper waved as she drove past to a parking spot. She quickly parked and hustled to join them.

"Now, I don't want any of you to feel inhibited. Get whatever you want on the menu, and don't worry about it. We all worked hard this year and deserve a treat," Joshua said as they hurried inside.

The sky had clouded over and looked like piles of dirty cotton balls. The temperature had dropped since that morning, and the wind that had picked up sought out any exposed part of their bodies. Maggie was wrapped up tight in a padded coat that made her look like a caterpillar. Casper was still wearing his Santa hat. Babs had a leather jacket like a greaser from the fifties zipped up tight and a red scarf wound all the way around her blond locks and across her mouth.

Joshua shuffled in behind everyone, his hands thrust deep in his coat pockets, his head completely uncovered, and his chin tucked into his chest. Once inside, he rubbed his hands together and walked up to the hostess, and before Maggie knew it, they were sitting at a high table for four with warm cider in front of everyone. A fireplace roared to the left. Beautiful red, white, and green Christmas ornaments hung from the ceiling. Pinecones and lush greenery covered almost every flat surface. In the corner across from the fireplace was a Christmas tree that almost reached the ceiling. Its delicate white lights twinkled as if they were winking at everyone.

Over the speakers, Maggie could hear the familiar notes of the Vince Guaraldi Trio, which brought her back to her childhood for just a few minutes. Everyone was talking, even Casper, who was usually so quiet. Joshua had many people coming up to shake his hand and say hello, promising to stop by the bookstore before the holiday. That was one of the drawbacks of owning a business on Main Street. Everyone knew who he was and wanted to talk to him. Maggie was more than happy to sit back and listen, taking note of all the people who came by while enjoying the yarns being spun by her coworkers.

"This is such a beautiful time of year. I just can't help but feel terrible for that Kylie Thornson," Babs said. "She's got a young son. This holiday is going to be hard."

"I'm glad Mr. Campbell had an alibi," Maggie said. "I like him."

"Isn't he right out of the pages of a Louis L'Amour novel?" Babs asked, impressing Maggie with her literary reference. "He really is a good man. Roy has talked to him on more than one occasion because they both have Harleys. He's just a good ol' boy."

"I heard he had a long record," Casper said. "He makes me nervous."

"People do stupid things when they are young," Maggie added.

"Isn't that the truth. Mine went by the name Jedidiah Holmes." Babs shook her head and clicked her tongue. "What was I thinking?"

Appetizers were ordered. Another round of

cider found its way to the table along with a Shirley Temple for Maggie. Everyone ordered some kind of steak, and Maggie couldn't help but think that it was the best food she'd ever tasted. Outside, the sun had started to set by the time they were all finished, and the Christmas party in the main dining room could be heard in the bar.

Casper and Babs had finished their meal and were ready to leave.

"I can't eat another bite," Babs said, patting her stomach. Casper had the same sentiment.

Before Maggie could do anything, they each gave her a big hug and said good-bye, leaving her alone with Joshua.

"Well, would you like another Shirley Temple? Maybe a coffee or a shot of Jägermeister?" Joshua teased. He had been with Maggie on the one and only night she had done a shot of hard liquor. It had resulted in an embarrassing kiss that Maggie pretended not to remember.

"I'm good. I think I'll use the ladies' room and then get going," she said.

"Are you sure? Maybe we could go somewhere and hear some music or have a hot cocoa or something," Joshua suggested.

"Maybe. I mean, only if you want to." She pushed her glasses up and twisted her mouth.

"I wouldn't have suggested it if I didn't want to," Joshua replied.

"If you are too tired or something, that's okay. I totally understand," Maggie insisted as she slid off the high stool.

"Just go to the bathroom, and I'll figure out someplace to go." Joshua shook his head and chuckled.

"I don't think I like your tone," Maggie needled.

"I don't like yours either," he snapped back with a grin.

Maggie arched her right eyebrow and smirked as she looked over her glasses at him. How dare he tease her like that while looking so handsome and being so generous?

"You certainly have a smart response to everything, don't you." She tried not to smile but failed when Joshua laughed. She shook her head and walked up to the hostess to ask where the powder room was.

"Just down this hallway and to the right," the hostess replied, pointing down a hallway that passed by the dining room and the loud Christmas party that was taking place there.

As Maggie walked past, she looked up and saw a familiar face in the crowd: Gretchen Armstrong. Gretchen didn't notice Maggie, as she was busy talking with a couple of men in suits. Obviously, this was the Christmas party for the law firm David Thornson had worked at. No one seemed to be too broken up that he wasn't there.

Maggie continued walking to the bathroom. After a few minutes, she walked back toward the bar but was cut short. The hostess had waved to one of the people in the law office's party. A large man with slicked-back hair suddenly appeared and took a folded piece of paper from the hostess. Maggie recognized the man. He had been standing in front of her car the night before.

Her breath hitched in her throat, and she turned around, pretending to admire a couple of Christmas decorations on the wall. Would he recognize her? She wasn't bundled up like she had been yesterday.

Whatever was in that note must not have been good news. As Maggie watched out of the corner of her eye, she saw him crumple up the note then dash back to a table to grab the same long tan coat he'd been wearing last night. He spoke with a different man in a suit before heading toward the door.

Maggie ran to Joshua, who was pulling his coat on when he saw her.

"He's here," she said. She grabbed her scarf and started winding it around her neck.

"Who?" Joshua looked over his shoulder.

"The guy from last night. He was in that party in the dining room. It's for the law firm that David Thornson worked at. Come on. I know where we can go." Maggie pulled her coat on.

"Oh, no. You think tailing this guy is a good idea? You're nuts, Maggie," Joshua said.

"Fine. Stay here. I'm going to follow him. He's up to something. He's tied to Kylie somehow, and her husband was shot in an ice shack. Is that a coincidence?" Maggie huffed as she yanked on her mittens and started toward the door.

Outside, the sun had already set. Christmas lights on the surrounding buildings and distant houses glowed beautifully against the black backdrop.

"The police are handling this. They'll find who killed David Thornson. That's their job," Joshua said. He stood and started to put his jacket on.

"Are you coming?" Maggie looked over her glasses.

He zipped up his coat, shaking his head the whole time. "Fine. But I'm not…"

Maggie had already turned toward the door and was out in the cold while Joshua was still searching for his keys. Maggie pointed to the corner of the parking lot, where the barrel-chested man was climbing behind the wheel of a Mercedes.

"Hurry! We're going to lose him!" Maggie tugged Joshua's sleeve.

"We better take my car. He knows your car," Joshua said, making Maggie nod in agreement.

Within minutes, they were following the Mercedes back toward the direction of the book-store. Suddenly, Maggie was sure she knew where this guy was going. After a few twists and turns, he made his way down a familiar street. Everything was quiet except one building.

Chapter 21

"Find a place to park," Maggie instructed. "He's going to the brownstone."

"It looks like that's where everyone is going," Joshua said.

It was a complete transformation from the scary, haunted-looking place Maggie had snuck into the night before. People wearing fancier coats and carrying gift bags were walking up the front stoop into the brownstone. Soft, warm lights shone through the slats of boarded-up windows.

"This is peculiar. Well, straighten your hair and sweater," Maggie said.

"And?" Joshua asked.

"And let's go in," Maggie said while unhooking her seatbelt.

"You want to crash the party?"

Maggie turned around in her seat and saw the man with slicked-back hair stomping toward the brownstone as if he was going to war.

"I think the speedometer said we were going about sixty miles an hour in a forty-mile-an-hour zone. He's in a hurry." She pointed to the figure hurrying to the front steps. "I bet I know why. I'll bet Kylie is in there." Maggie shook her head.

"Maggie, you are starting to get into the habit of leading me to places that aren't safe. If we have another incident like we did at Little Al's place… well, that wasn't all bad," Joshua teased.

Maggie's eyes bugged, and her cheeks glowed with embarrassment before she got out of the car. Joshua had to trot to catch up with her. When he finally did at the front of the brownstone, they could hear Christmas music, chatter, and laughing.

Maggie led Joshua up to the house, down the gangway, and through the bent chain-link fence.

"What are we doing back here? Why aren't we going in through the front door like normal people?" Joshua asked.

"Because we want to blend in. It's better this way," Maggie insisted.

The back door was unlocked, as it had been

before. As soon as they stepped in, they saw that a bustling makeshift kitchen had been set up in the midst of the original one. Finger food and glasses of champagne were being carried out to the other rooms.

Joshua grabbed Maggie's hand and, with her head tucked down, led her straight through the kitchen and down the hallway.

"Blend in? If you had stood there much longer, they would have known we didn't belong," Joshua whispered as they stood in the hallway.

Space heaters gave the rooms a pleasant temperature. Speakers had been rigged in the corners and were piping out jazzy tunes. The guests looked as if they were all having a lovely time, sipping champagne and chatting about anything and everything.

"There." Maggie pulled Joshua closer and pointed across the room. "That's Kylie. And will you look at who's with her?"

"Who is it?" Joshua stretched his neck.

"That's the mystery man from the other night. She doesn't look like she's holding his hand or anything. Who is that guy?" Then Maggie grabbed Joshua's arm.

"What is it?"

"There's our friend from the restaurant. He looks like he did when he was in front of my car last night—angry," Maggie said.

She and Joshua watched him elbow his way between two guests to get at Kylie. He whispered something in her ear. Whatever it was caused Kylie to excuse herself from the group as well as her mystery man and walk away with the barrel-chested man following close behind.

"We've got to hear what they are saying," Maggie said before chewing her bottom lip.

"That means we have to blend in. Your words." Joshua smirked. "Follow my lead." Maggie didn't have time to put up a fight. Joshua slipped one arm around her waist and pulled her into the lively room. With the other, he grabbed her a glass of champagne.

"I can't drink. You know that," she muttered angrily.

"Take it and pretend," Joshua replied.

They smiled, and Joshua babbled on about the structure of the brick walls and the decorations that made the scary building look downright cozy, and in between it all, he managed to weave them through the crowd. Before Maggie could put up a fuss, they were just outside a small cubby in which

Kylie and the big man were having a not-so-private conversation.

Maggie reached for Joshua's arm but found his hand instead. He locked his fingers through hers. Together, they slipped into the darkness and listened.

"He was cheating on you, Kylie. I told you that," the man with the slicked-back hair and long tan coat said.

"It was none of your business. *This* is none of your business. I have every right to do what I'm doing, and you need to just stop this, George," Kylie pleaded.

"I can give you anything you want. You want this broken-down old building? I'll give it to you. You want your father to continue living with you? We can make that work. Just say it, Kylie, and I'll do anything for you. You know that. Haven't I proved I'll do *anything* for you?"

"George, what are you saying?" Kylie asked.

"He was cheating on you with someone in the office. He was making a fool of you, and I just couldn't stand by and let him do that," George said.

"What did you do, George?"

"Come on, Kylie. As if making you look like a complete idiot wasn't enough, he had a drinking problem. I knew how he talked to you. Everyone did. Just like everyone knew you didn't deserve it. What you ever saw in him to begin with still…"

"George, my relationship with my husband was none of your business or anyone else's. If you did what I think you did…George…you have to go to the police." Kylie choked the words out.

"No, I don't. They have a suspect in mind. A guy with a record who lives like a recluse and had a serious problem with your deceased husband. It's perfect. No one would believe George Allis of Allis, Blum, and Thornson would kill anyone," he said and laughed. "There is only one tiny loose end that I need your help with. Just a tiny thing really."

"Don't you hear yourself? You sound like a crazy person. Please, tell me this is just one of your dramatic performances. Please don't tell me you did it. That you killed…"

"That I killed David Thornson?" George said. "I did the world a favor, and you know it."

"Yeah, that's what everyone is going to think. That I knew about it. George, what have you done?" Kylie's voice trembled.

"You don't have to worry. I will make sure that it all goes away. If you'll just…" George's words sounded like they were coated in grease. Slimy, slithery words that passed as one thing but really meant another.

"If I'll just what?"

"Just do as I say and…"

"The days of my being told what to do are over, George. Our affair meant nothing!" Kylie snapped.

Maggie gasped before clapping her hand on her own mouth. Her eyes bugged as she looked at Joshua, who was also hooked on the conversation.

"An affair?" Maggie mouthed the words. She gawked at Joshua, who shrugged and shook his head in response before leaning in to continue listening.

"You don't mean that," George insisted.

He didn't come across as the kind of guy who took no for an answer. In fact, if Maggie had had to guess, it was probably something he never heard, especially from pretty, petite women.

"But I do. And you should know that. I tried to be like David. I tried not to care and just build my own separate life while married to him. What better way to get back at a cheating husband than to cheat on him? That was what I thought. And to add salt to the wound, the partner of his law firm. It sounded good at the time, George," Kylie said.

"It was good. It *is* good," George insisted.

"No. It isn't. It's as sleazy as it was when David was alive," Kylie replied.

Maggie pressed her back against the wall and slowly peeked around the doorframe. She watched as Kylie dropped her head and slumped as if she were just exhausted.

But then George pounced. He grabbed Kylie by the arms and shook her hard.

"After everything I've done for you, you are not going to leave me like this," he hissed just inches from her face.

"You're hurting me." Kylie winced.

"If you don't verify my alibi and then join me, I'll make sure you not only don't get this brownstone for a bed-and-breakfast but that you don't get the buyout of David's share of the law firm. You could use that money, I know. Because he ran up your debt. You decide, Kylie," George growled before letting her go.

Kylie rubbed her arms, her head hanging low.

"You think these people are here because they like you? They're here because I told them to come."

"That's not true," Kylie whimpered.

"Sure it is. You'll only stay afloat if you stay with me. I'll give you everything you want, Kylie.

All I ask is for you to help me clear up these loose ends. Then everything will be perfect."

Maggie watched as George smoothed Kylie's hair before she tried to pull away.

"What loose ends?"

"Your husband's datebook. I'll need that. You'll have to get it from your friend," George said. He straightened his tie and ran his hand over his slicked-back hair.

"What friend?"

"That nerdy girl with the glasses. She went into David's ice shack and got it. The reason I know this is because I was there to get it. I saw her leave with it, and then she showed up at your house," George said.

"I have no idea who you are talking about," Kylie said.

"She was just at your house the other day. Don't lie, Kylie. You just don't know how to do it." George rolled his eyes.

"No one has been at my house. It's just been my dad and Leo and me. With everything that's gone on, I…wait. You mean the girl with the House Decorating Committee?" Kylie shook her head. "That's the only person to come to the door."

"Come on, Kylie. I know you a little better than that," George huffed.

"You don't know me at all. You think you do because we had one fling when I was feeling so alone that I wanted to die. But you don't know me at all. Please, George. Tell me you didn't do what you said you did. Tell me I heard you wrong. That you were just trying to impress me but that you really didn't hurt David," Kylie pleaded.

"Maybe I should have killed you instead of David. At least he was making me money," George said cruelly.

Just then, in the other room, a couple gasps and yelps cut through the merriment, making Maggie and Joshua turn and stare.

Chapter 22

"Excuse me! Excuse me!" a man in a trench coat called out, holding up a badge as he and another man dressed almost identically pushed their way through the crowd.

Behind them was Gary, who, upon seeing Maggie, shook his head as if it was no surprise to see her there.

She shrugged and stepped out of the way.

"You!"

Maggie heard the word, but it didn't register for a second that it had been directed at her. She slowly turned her head to the left, looking directly into the small room Kylie and George were in. Kylie looked at Maggie with a confused expression as if she was flipping through the Rolodex of faces in her memory.

Maggie didn't much worry about that. It was the raging glare from George that made Maggie shake where she was standing.

"You! You were following me! Officer, arrest this woman!" He pointed a thick finger at Maggie. "She's been stalking me, harassing me for days. I'm in fear for my life."

"What?" Maggie shouted.

"Nice try, Counselor. George Allis, you are under arrest for embezzlement, blackmail, and, oh yeah, the murder of David Thornson. Place your hands behind your back," the flatfoot said.

"This is some kind of mistake." George straightened and smirked at the detectives. "If we can go back to my office, I'm sure we can straighten this out."

"You have the right to remain silent," the flatfoot said.

By now, everyone had stopped what they were doing and begun gawking.

"I told you that you were making a mistake. Kylie, tell them about us. Straighten all this out, please." George looked at Kylie, who had tears in her eyes.

That was when Gary pushed past everyone. "You did a good job, Mrs. Thornson. We got it all on tape. Are you all right?" he asked her.

Kylie glared at George before reaching into the top of her dress and pulling out a wire.

"And I'll bet that little brat was in cahoots with you the whole time!" George shouted, pointing at Maggie.

"Me?" Maggie gulped. "Don't look at me, pal."

"Mags, maybe you should come with me as well," Gary said.

He let the detectives attempt to cuff George. The lawyer backed up farther into the room, holding his hands up while shaking his head. When they tried to take hold of him, George Allis started swinging and cursing. Just as Maggie looked away, they crashed into a wall, sending a shower of powdered plaster down on all their heads.

"What is going on?" Maggie asked.

Gary politely passed Kylie off to one of the female uniformed officers on the scene, who had been holding the crowd of gawkers back.

The Christmas music still played. From the

kitchen, the clamor of plates and pots and pans and a soft murmur of conversation could still be heard. The guests looked around at each other, at Maggie and Joshua, and tried to see the chaos that was taking place in the small room, where detectives were still trying to cuff Mr. Allis.

"Everyone, the drinks are still cold and the food is still hot, and it's a beautiful night for a get-together. Please, we'll explain everything if you'll just step back and let the police do their job," Kylie's mystery man said. He turned his back on the excitement and urged the guests to spread out for the police.

Maggie looked at Gary.

"Joshua, did she convince you to come along snooping?" Gary asked.

"Yes. Yes, she did," Joshua replied. "I don't think any time we've ever been out in public there hasn't been some kind of embarrassing incident."

"Yeah, that sort of thing follows Maggie around." Gary chuckled.

"If you two want to stop swapping recipes, maybe you could tell me what in the world is going on in there." Maggie jerked her thumb toward where the detectives and George Allis were having their brawl. It was as if the running of the bulls was taking place in that tiny, unfurnished room.

"Let's get out of here. The detectives should have Mr. Allis under control in a minute. They've got backup outside. We can slip out by the kitchen," Gary said.

Maggie followed Gary and Joshua and listened as Joshua told her oldest and dearest friend what she'd been up to the previous night. She felt as if she was being reported to the principal.

They stepped out onto the back stoop, where giant snowflakes had started to fall. The temperature had warmed, making it perfect snow shower weather, and the wind had died down. The warm lights shone through the slats of wood over the windows and the crack in the door, making patterns on the ground.

"Maggie, I think I'm going to have to request a monitoring ankle bracelet for you that prevents you from going anywhere other than home and the bookshop." Gary shook his head and put his hands on his hips.

"I was just curious. Why do you think the world is in such a state? Not enough people ask questions, that's why."

"And what did you find out, smarty pants?" Gary asked as he tilted his head to the right.

"David Thornson was having an affair with Gretchen Armstrong in his office. And written in his calendar, he listed every time he met up with her, including the night he was murdered. So…"

"So?" Gary asked.

"So, Kylie was home with her father and son as an alibi so her mystery man could…"

"Her what?" Gary asked.

"Her mystery man," Maggie explained. "The guy who was at the Ice Fishing Jubilee Dance and who was in there right now, but you walked right past him." Maggie huffed and put her hands on her hips.

"That *mystery man* is Kylie's cousin, Nate Habertieg. He's in real estate. He helped her buy this place so she could turn it into a bed-and-breakfast," Gary replied, his forehead wrinkled by his eyebrows pushing upward.

"Maggie, you were all wrong on this one." Joshua snickered.

"No, I wasn't. I didn't know who Mr. Habertieg was, but the conversation I'd overheard led me to believe that he had done something to David Thornton. However, Mr. Allis was the shape that has been following me all over town. It was only a matter of time before I would have figured out that he was responsible for David's death. I wouldn't have had to hear him confess it. I would have figured it out," Maggie replied and stuck her tongue out at both Joshua and Gary.

"The real story is this," Gary said. "Kylie moved here with David not even a year ago. It was obvious that he'd been, well, rather mean to her. I'll just say that."

Maggie put her arms down and wrapped them around herself. "What did he do to her?"

Gary looked over his shoulder then back at Maggie. "She came into the police station with bruises. She admitted that her husband had done it but that she wasn't going to press charges. It was sad to hear her speak, but she wasn't confident the law would lock him up long enough for her to get her life back. Instead, she told us about the questionable practices between her husband, Gretchen Armstrong, and George Allis," Gary said. "We agreed to help her, but this was dealing with big money and high-end clients and the City of Boston, so we had to get them involved. That's why they are taking Mr. Allis into custody and not me."

"Gretchen Armstrong? She was having an affair with David," Maggie said.

"How did you know that?" Joshua interrupted.

"I did a little research. Jeez." Maggie rolled her eyes.

"We know. The thing about women like Gretchen is that they will do almost anything for money, but they'll do even more than that for freedom. She was threatened with jail time as an accomplice. She spilled the beans on both of them," Gary replied. "Plus, it wasn't her that David was seeing in his calendar that you handed over. It was meetings with George Allis. George was meeting David on the night he was murdered. They weren't the best at covering their tracks. But they were lawyers. Not always as smart as they think they are."

"What about Kylie's affair with Allis? Is she going to be in trouble for that? Does that make her part of the whole conspiracy?" Joshua asked.

"It isn't against the law to step out on your spouse. Kylie told us about it. It wasn't really an affair. They were together one time before Kylie came to us. She was desperate. She wanted to hurt her husband like he'd hurt her. Except it didn't work out that way. When she told David, he did nothing more than call her names, but he wouldn't let her go. He took away her allowance and left her without a car most of the time as he went about doing his own thing," Gary replied.

The noises inside the house were getting louder. "Maybe you should go in there and help," Joshua suggested to Gary.

"They have their own officers with them," Gary said as he looked at the door. "Yeah, maybe I should just offer to…"

Before Gary could take a step forward and finish his sentence, the back door thundered as someone crashed into it from the other side. Almost tearing the door off the hinges was the hulking form of George Allis, his eyes red and wild, his face drenched in sweat, his tie loosed and dangling around his neck like a noose that had snapped instead of tightening. His jacket was half off, and his hair had fallen into a disheveled mop on top of his head.

The fit of hysterics had him charging out the door, knocking Joshua to the ground and Gary into the other plank of plywood that was covering the other door. In his haste to get away from the Boston detectives, he collided with Maggie, sending them both flying off the back stoop and onto the snow-covered ground at the bottom of it. Maggie gasped and choked as she tried to catch the breath that had been knocked out of her. She lay on her back, looking up at the black sky as white flakes floated down, melting instantly on her cheeks.

George Allis wasn't much better off. He lay sprawled out as if he'd had the idea of making snow angels. He wheezed, unable to gulp down enough breath to get a second wind, as the detectives, looking as if they'd just gone twelve rounds with a heavyweight boxer defending his title, sprinted down the back steps.

"Nice try, Georgie!" one of them yelled, and he brought a knee up and onto George's chest.

"Roll him over, Cos. I got the cuffs," the other detective shouted before kneeling next to his partner.

All the fight had left George as soon as he hit the ground. At first, as Maggie rolled to the side to get out of the way, she thought the man was choking. But then she heard the loud, pathetic wail and realized George Allis, the stampeding rhino who had looked so terrifying the night before, was crying. Crying like a baby.

"Maggie!" Joshua shouted.

"Jeez, Maggie! What are you trying to do?"

Gary chimed in. Both men came to her aid, each offering her a hand to get up.

"Looks like if it wasn't for me, your perp would have gotten away," Maggie said as she rubbed her tailbone.

"Yeah, that's it," Gary grumbled. "You stopped *the perp*. Do me a favor and don't use police jargon."

"Are you kidding me? He'd be halfway to Boston by now if I hadn't used my body as a weapon." She looked from Gary to Joshua and back to Gary.

"What do you say we go get some coffee or something, Gary? I've had enough parties and excitement to last me until next Christmas," Joshua said.

"You said a mouthful, Josh. Do you mind driving? I came with the guys from Boston," Gary replied as he and Joshua headed toward the door.

"What about me?" Maggie asked. "I think I broke my bippy."

"Broke your bippy. Yeah, you did." Joshua offered her his elbow.

Maggie slipped her hand into the crook of his arm and grabbed Gary to do the same with him.

"You said coffee? At the shop?" Maggie asked.

"Yeah. Think you can manage to stay out of trouble until then?" Joshua asked.

"Hey," Maggie huffed. "I don't think I like your tone." She wrinkled her nose and squinted.

"Don't make me have to split you two up," Gary said. "Maggie, I think you better ride in the back seat."

Chapter 23

Cars were lined up along the street for almost two blocks surrounding Babs's house. Maggie parked, grabbed the bottle of sparkling grape juice and bouquet of red and white carnations, and climbed out of the car. For the first time in recent memory, she didn't feel like a worm on a hook being lowered into a tank of piranha.

Babs's neighborhood was a lot different from where Maggie called home. The houses appeared to be in a contest as to who could decorate with the tackiest lights possible. The address she was looking for would have been impossible to miss. Not only was the music audible at the end of the block, but a group of people had congregated on the stoop, smoking cigarettes and chatting pleasantly as they sipped from beer bottles or small plastic cups.

It felt as if it took Maggie ten minutes to get from the front door to the kitchen, where she saw Babs at the counter, laughing and talking as she assembled what looked like mini meatball sandwiches.

"I don't think I'd recognize you if you weren't at a counter," Maggie teased.

"Maggie!" Babs squealed before giving her a big hug and a hearty merry Christmas. Within minutes, Maggie had been introduced to cousins, neighbors, ex-wives, new husbands, and more than a dozen children, who ran past fueled by the excitement that Santa would be coming in a few more days.

"Do you need some help?" Maggie offered.

"No. I've got it all under control. Joshua, Casper, and his little girlfriend are in the basement, playing darts or pool or something. Why don't you go ahead. I'm bringing these down in a second." Babs nodded toward the meatball sandwiches, which smelled so good Maggie's stomach growled. She was thankful the sound of music and a football game on television drowned it out.

Roy was there with his sidekick, Earl, strapped to his chest as usual. He gave Maggie a sideways hug as he took her coat. Earl was sleeping through all the noise and commotion. Roy promised to be down soon, as they were going to crank up the karaoke machine.

Maggie shivered at the thought but went downstairs anyway. There were just as many people downstairs as upstairs. People said hello as she squeezed by, looking for her friends. Overhead, hundreds of beautiful vintage ornaments in every color hung from the ceiling. Old couches and chairs filled the place, and every flat surface had platters of food or a mini bar set up on it. Elvis sang "Blue Christmas" as a handful of couples danced, while everyone else continued talking and having a good time.

If she'd had to choose between the two parties —Kylie Thornson's elegant event or this party— there would be no contest. Maggie wouldn't have cared even if she hadn't been meeting her friends. The atmosphere was friendly and welcoming. But she was grateful when she saw Joshua standing behind a card table, waving her over.

There you go again, looking handsome and confident, she thought. She gave an awkward wave and tugged at her Christmas sweater. It was a vintage cardigan with intricate beadwork along the front.

If anyone looked closely, they might see that a couple of strands were coming undone, but it was too beautiful to hide just because it had one small flaw.

"Mags! Glad you are here! We need a fourth player," Joshua said as he pulled a folding chair from against the wall behind him. "I've been hoarding this chair since I got here." With a yank, he snapped the chair open and placed it next to him.

"Merry Christmas, Maggie," Casper said. He introduced his girlfriend, Shayla. She seemed like a nice girl as far as teenagers went.

Maggie sat down carefully, as if she might be walking into a trap.

"We've got a cutthroat game of Go Fish going on here. Are you in?" Joshua asked.

"Go Fish? I actually know the rules to that card game. Count me in," Maggie replied.

Casper dealt a new hand for everyone, and before long, the rules were being argued, accusations of cheating were flying, and Maggie was laughing so hard her stomach hurt.

"I had good luck before you sat down, Mags! What are you doing to me?" Joshua teased.

"Maybe this game is just a little too difficult for

you," Maggie razzed back, smiling. "Where can I get something to drink? I'm thirsty."

"I'll get you something, Maggie. Shayla, would you like to help me?" Casper asked his girlfriend. He stood and offered her his hand like a real gentleman.

Shayla smiled broadly and nodded.

"They make a cute couple, don't they," Maggie said as she watched Casper take Shayla's hand.

He whispered something in her ear, making her laugh.

"They do," Joshua said, but his tone of voice sounded different. She looked at him and found that he wasn't watching Casper and Shayla. He was looking at her.

"Have you gotten all of your Christmas shopping done?" Maggie asked nervously, looking down and tugging at the sleeves of her dress.

"Just about. You haven't told me what you want for Christmas," Joshua said.

"Me? Oh, you gave me a bonus and took us out for lunch. I don't think I had to eat for three days after that because I was so full." Maggie smiled.

"You don't want a piece of jewelry or something for your house? I'd be happy to get something for you. Or maybe it will be Santa who brings you something," Joshua said.

Maggie's heart was racing. What was the matter with her? Joshua was just her boss, making small talk about Christmas gifts. He wasn't down on one knee with a diamond ring in a velvet box. She could tell him that she would have loved a new brooch from an antique shop or maybe a vintage tablecloth and napkins with some pretty birds or a monogram hand-stitched on them.

"I don't really need anything," Maggie said.

"It's not about needing, Maggie. It's about wanting to spread the joy of the season." Joshua smiled and looked deeply into her eyes.

Just then, Casper and Shayla returned with drinks in their hands.

"Sorry, Mags. They didn't have any cherry grenadine. But they had cherry Coke. I hope that works for you," Casper said and handed her a plastic cup filled with soda.

She smiled at the fact that he'd remembered the Shirley Temple that she had drunk at their Christmas lunch. She thanked him just as a whole bunch of commotion started at the end of the room.

Babs and Roy made a grand entrance. She was

carrying a huge tray of meatball sandwiches, and he had a huge bowl filled with an antipasti salad that looked delicious. They placed the food on a long buffet next to the card table, and Maggie was glad. She wanted to load up a plate, take her drink, sit in a corner, and savor every bite as she watched the partygoers having a wonderful time.

"We're putting on the karaoke machine!" Roy shouted, making everyone burst out in cheers and applause.

"Karaoke is a tradition at my house," Babs said to Maggie as she pulled an old-fashioned Polaroid camera from a shelf. "Just like this is."

It took nothing to get all of her family and friends to assemble for a quick picture. They posed with their tongues hanging out, bunny ears behind each other's heads, and plenty of broad smiles. When she got to Casper and Shayla, there was no need to ask them twice to pose close together.

"Aren't they cute?" Joshua said to Maggie.

She had a mouth full of food. "Mmmhmm." She nodded and dabbed the corners of her lips with a napkin before speaking. "Remember being that young and feeling that way?"

"What are you talking about? You don't have to be young to feel that way," Joshua said and gave her that look again. That look that had her feeling like the canary being sized up by the cat. Except that the cat was pretty.

"Now you two!" Babs shouted. "Let me get a picture."

Maggie set her food down and sat with her back straight and her hands properly in her lap.

"No, Maggie, I want to get your whole outfit. Your outfits always remind me of those proper ladies from the fifties. You and Joshua stand over there. That way, I can get your whole ensemble," Babs instructed, and there was no arguing with her.

"How about by the record player, Babs?" Maggie suggested. "That way, the old-fashioned record player will add to the composition."

"Good idea," Babs said and winked.

Maggie walked over to the old Victrola, and Joshua followed close behind. They struck a pose on either side of the machine as it played "White Christmas" by Bing Crosby.

"You guys look great. But you better look up," Roy said as he walked up to Babs's side.

"What?" Maggie said.

"Look up." Babs pointed.

When Maggie looked up, she felt all the air rush out of her body. Above their heads hung a beautifully bunched bouquet of mistletoe. How could she not have seen it dangling there all by itself in the small square of space where people had, moments ago, been dancing and carrying on like nothing was out of the ordinary? When all the while, overhead was the plant that had struck fear into her heart, hanging there as if it had been waiting all night for this opportunity.

Joshua, who had glanced up and smiled now, looked at Maggie as if he was certain she was going to not just blush a thousand different shades of red but maybe faint.

But she didn't do either of those things. Instead, Maggie chuckled, squared her shoulders, and leaned over for Joshua to kiss her cheek. When his lips touched her skin, she felt a rush of heat. But she didn't buckle or flinch. Instead, she turned and looked him straight in the eyes.

"Merry Christmas, Joshua."

"You sure have made it one. Merry Christmas, Maggie."

About the Author

Harper Lin is a *USA TODAY* bestselling cozy mystery author. When she's not reading or writing mysteries, she loves going to yoga classes, hiking, and hanging out with her family and friends.

For a complete list of her books by series, visit her website. Follow Harper on social media using the icons below for the latest insider news.

www.HarperLin.com